The Sky Above

A.G.R. Goff

Also, by A.G.R. Goff
Layers

Visit the author:
www.agr-goff.com
Twitter @AGR_Goff
Instagram agr_goff
or Facebook agrgoff

For Moritz
Wherever you are

It doesn't matter why it happened in 2021 and what it was called. The names varied: Great wave of migration, migrant stream, most serious refugee influx since World War II, great replacement. When Europe declared it wasn't able to accept any more refugees, the world burned. I still cannot figure out how politicians didn't see it coming. Nothing happened overnight. Years went by. Anybody with half a brain cell predicted it. What followed was the disintegration of the modern, western world within the space of a few weeks. One event followed another, starting everywhere around the world, finding their climax in Europe, like a house of cards collapsing by the blow of a sudden wind. It didn't start with the attacks in Manchester or the Brexit. But it's the events I recall most because I was old enough to understand we moved backwards. The atomic bombs detonated much later, and they were the ultimate blow. Explosives deployed for many years, in the Middle East and Asia. But nobody in the West cared until it reached us in Madrid, London, and New York. Even when atomic bombs detonated, we counted on it not shattering our Western world. Our government would catch the bad guys, and things would go back to normal. A few thousand people would die far away, somewhere abroad. But they didn't. The explosions at the Eiffel Tower, the Oktoberfest and Big Ben - all at the same time- were the final straw for starting a religious civil war, waiting to kick off for years. Conceivably it was purely another attack, but somehow these events were the most talked about ones. People were fed up. Maybe it wasn't only about spirituality, but it didn't matter now. I remember other explosions during the cause of that day, but they drowned in the reporting about these three significant hallmarks of civilisation. For a minute everything was silent and then hell broke loose. Looters, rapists, brutes - all the scum and waste human societies produced controlled the streets under the pretence of trying to protect what was left of western civilisation. People beat others because of the colour of their skin. White, black or Asian, it didn't matter. The attacks in Paris, Munich and London were only an excuse for people to vent their frustrations. There was always someone with too much aggression. Shop windows were smashed; tinned and preserved food was gone within days. The final explosion covered everything in ash. The city was dead, a zombie. Somehow still moving, but not living. Hope, the backbone of society disappeared. But people kept going. England deserted back to the times before the industrial revolution. Well, at least it looked that way. A major newspaper, still running, reported that the plague and other unnamed diseases had made a comeback. The towns and roads, the rotting farms and abandoned cars showed no signs of survival. Fear ruled, and people stayed hidden. Cholera struck because of unclean water. But at least it hit everybody - the innocent and the guilty. By that time, I was ready to accept that I was going to die, starve to death or die from lack of clean water. But everything changed when I saw there was hope. It was like a rare flower growing in a cellar, moving towards a small light source.

I learned it wasn't too late when I met him years after the last big events. He was a doctor, and maybe I was his first patient. The man didn't realise he was a healer not being qualified in the traditional sense. But he was keen to learn. Much later he would live with the damned, a group of vulnerable and sick people isolated in Epping Forest. But I was long gone at that point. Maybe it was me who made him assume he could support people. He couldn't stop me from dying, but I gave the doctor hope. I couldn't understand why nobody had attacked them and stolen their food and water, but that would soon change when I looked at the facts. The forest protected them and much later when he became the doctor, nobody wanted to catch whatever they carried. And they didn't care about spirituality or politics. People were living together and, when I watched them from above, I realised they were one of the few self-sustaining groups who survived and would shape the future. He was their unelected leader and the main force behind the only thing that could make everybody heal and forgive. It was this remarkable man who taught everybody it didn't matter what you believed in as long as you accepted there were others who deserved the right to live different. He brought people together, took away their fear, helped them rebuilt their shattered lives from the ruins of doctrine and their belief in knowing the only truth. I'm an old soul and have been old since the disease digged its ugly fingers into my skin. There is no fighting spirit left. I'm only waiting to move on. Maybe it is something spiritual. I don't know for sure. I haven't seen it. But the fact I'm here tells me this isn't the end. It's 2045, and I'm only sure about one thing. If there is a god, he or she doesn't care. It will just watch. The world is different now. Sure, they rebuild what they could. And if someone looks at them it would seem like not much has changed. They still use computers, cars and technology. But it's very different. They only seem to appreciate everything that little bit more. People don't buy new mobile phones every year. Advertising and commercials are a thing of the past. Instead, they produce what they need. The sky above sparkles with stars every night, uninterrupted by artificial lights. The few cars are not enough to compete. All of this would not have been possible without him. He shaped it by giving up clinging to the past. He just pushed up his sleeves. I admire his will, his resilience and that he never tried to point fingers. It would only make things worse. I guess what I worship above all is his common sense. But all he has achieved is in danger again. People don't focus on the good he's done. They take it for granted once again, blaming others and search for comfort in a fantasy world. Once again, they don't accept responsibility and hope for a better afterlife. They have not learned from the past but destroyed the future. Someone wrote his name in the books of history, but nobody seems to read them except me.

Clifford McDormick
6 February 2045

Chapter 1

18th of September 2021 London Shepards Bush-Tunis Road
The day everything changed
Mark

When Mark woke up at night from the cold reaching out, touching his toes uncovered by his blanket, he sensed something was different. He was only thirteen years old, but felt something significant was coming. His brother Brian was breathing in his sleep. It was dark beyond darkness and the day didn't want to come. Mark's hand rose to switch on his bedside lamp, but stopped because he didn't want to wake Brian. He pushed off his blue Batman blanket and raised himself up. He appreciated he was too old for superheroes, but it had always made him feel comfortable. Somehow it was different today. His bare feet touched the cold floor when he sat up, and he shivered. He heard noises and walked downstairs into the kitchen.

His mum and dad didn't hear him. They stared at the small flat-screen television in the middle of the room.

"Are you okay?" the boy said. His parents were like strangers. They didn't even bother to turn around. He rubbed the top of his left foot with his right one. They showed signs of turning into ice blocks. But it didn't seem to be important. His eyes focused on the television screen. There was fire, strange noises, people screaming.

A reporter stood stern facing a camera. "The bombings destroying the Eiffel Tower, injuring hundreds of people in Munich and London detonated at the same time. Two thousand five hundred sixty-seven people from around the world are dead so far. We have the biggest numbers of casualties confirmed in Paris. They injured many more in the attacks, but as of now, I can confirm no exact numbers. The toll does not include the eight terrorists who have died. The blasts occurred on the main platform of the Eiffel Tower, the Oktoberfest in Munich and Big Ben at 9 PM European time."

Mark remembered something like that happened in Manchester, a while ago. His mum and dad were very serious, but this was different. They looked like ghosts. He found it difficult to even glance at them and their blank faces. His eyes moved to the window. Herold, their skinny bushy-tailed cat, rose from his favourite place on the radiator, stretched and arched his back. Mark picked him up, stroking the pet absent-minded. He filled its bowl with milk, even though it was far too early. He wasn't aware of the time, but it was still dark outside. "Mum?" His voice sounded high and tinny. Nothing like the breaking voice of a teenager.

"Sorry?"

A reaction. Mark's heartbeat sped up. Things would be ok now. His mum just hadn't heard him.

She pulled her gaze away from the television screen and patted his head. "Why aren't you in bed, Darling? It is far too late."

"Mum, what's happening?"

She sighed and walked into the living room, feeding their angels and plecos in the tank. Mark didn't interrupt her even though it was the wrong time to feed the fish. His dad was still watching the news. Mark stood there, waiting.

His mum checked the tank's temperature. "I don't know", she said, more to herself than to anyone in particular.

"What don't you know?"

"What?" She turned around watching her son with glassy eyes.

"You said, you don't know. Mum, what's happening? It's these explosions, isn't it? You're worried because we're living in London, right?"

She didn't answer because Mark's dad walked into the living room.

"People are asking for the Royal Air Force or even the SAS to get involved. The American president wants to send troops and detonate an atomic bomb in North Korea. As if that would help. It has nothing to do with North Korea. The Russian president got involved. But he always comments. "We will regard any of this as an attack on Russian allies and therefore on Russia itself", he said. But it's only talks. I mean if you ask me, he's glad that the attention is on Europe and he can feign once more he is doing everything right in Russia. And the American, he rather sends his armies to London. It's far away, and he can pretend there are no problems in the U.S.A. But it wouldn't surprise me if there would be more explosions soon. Big ones. The ones here will be peanuts in comparison. This time they will go off somewhere in the States."

Mark's mum frowned. "Be careful what you say. You don't want to scare Mark."

The sounds of sirens interrupted them.

She took a deep breath. "Mark, where's Brian?"

"He's still upstairs, fast asleep. Don't worry. I understand what's going on here. I'm thirteen. We speak about these things in school. It's sad, but it has happened before. It's not the end of the world. Is that what the sirens are about?"

"Not the end of…" Mark's dad chuckled. "Not the end of the world, he says. I tell you something. Long before we moved here, before you and Brian were born, before I met your mother; I lived in a large house, with big windows and a massive fireplace. It was one of the biggest houses in the area. I assumed nothing happens to us there, and nobody could destroy it. Now, someone has broken its windows, nailed the doors shut with wooden planks, and it's overgrown by weed. It's a house that's over 200 years old, and now it's dying. I cannot go back and rebuild it. There's nothing left of this house. When I was a boy, I could see for miles right down to the river bank. I felt like a king. You know what destroyed it?"

Mark looked at him. "No, I mean I know you are from Bosnia, and there was a war. That's why you came to England."

It was as if his dad couldn't hear him. "Religion that's what destroyed my house. Religion creates hate towards people who think different. Well, at least the sort of religion that seems to become more and more powerful right now."

"You mean, Islam?" The boy asked with his high voice.

"No, not just Islam. Other religions as well. They move away from the original idea of tolerance and love."

"Milo, he's a bit young for this."

"Young? I was younger than him and was eleven when I lost my parents. The same year I moved to England with my aunt not knowing why I had lost my home and my family in an instant."

Mark's mouth was dry. He had heard toned down versions of this story before and he found about the Yugoslavian war from school. He looked up and into his father's eyes. "Will this happen here? Do you think our house will die like yours in Bosnia?"

His mother gasped. "Milo! You scared him."

He looked at her and shrugged. "Mark, come here. I need to explain something." Mark looked at him with wide eyes. "Don't worry. Sit down." The boy's legs buckled, and he fell into the red leather armchair, standing right next to him. His father kneeled in front of him. "I don't know what will happen. Maybe people will just rebuild everything and get on with their lives, and everything will be more or less how it has always been. Well, at least for us. But these explosions were massive. They killed a lot of people. But all depends on what people will do now. Remember that things you put into your mind are there forever. You might be able to push them aside for a while, but they will always come back. The negative and the positive. I mean, of course, you can forget some things? We all do. But it's not always like you want it to be. I mean, we forget what we want to remember, and we remember what we want to forget. The negative thoughts are very persistent. They just come creeping back, making you paranoid and that's what happens at the moment. People stare at each other, distrusting others who appear a certain way and that mistrust can turn into hate. That hate keeps you awake at night and makes you even more paranoid." The boy stared at his dad. With the small ceiling line shining on his skin his face looked striped and almost as if he was crying.

"Can I ask you something?" he whispered.

"Yes, sure."

"Are we going to die?"

"Milo?" Mark's mother cried out again.

"At some point, we all must die. But not now."

"So, I will still go to school tomorrow?"

"Yes."

"Okay."

But his dad had been wrong.

Chapter 2

Ross-on-Wye, Herefordshire
Five years later

On the far side of the river Wye, the road curled through black woods. Burned and leafless tree logs stretched to the sky as if pointing to something they couldn't reach. The road was muddy, and the drooping, rusty remains of barbed wire strung from scorched, telephone poles still lined up as a reminder of past times. Bright moonlight shone on the remains of a burned cottage, and beyond that, on a greyish mud bank created long ago for roadworks to go ahead. Further along one could see old signs showing the way to Abergavenny. Faded and weathered but still readable.

The man continued walking and just stopped when he needed to catch his breath. He said nothing at first, just listening to the cold wind and the trees whispering to each other. He looked at the girl by his side.

"I'm fine", the girl whispered. The man put his gloved hand on her shoulder and took another deep breath.

"Only a little more. It's not far." He nodded towards the ruins of the cottage but didn't move, just standing on the road.

"What?" the girl looked up at him.

"Nothing. Don't worry. There is nobody. No smoke, no lights. Can you see?"

"Yes. I can." The girl adjusted the rucksack on her back. "Are you sure it's ok? There's nobody to hurt us? Nobody?"

"Yes, it will be okay. A little more and we can go to sleep. We cannot make a fire. Okay? And we cannot use the lamp. But we can warm each other. Is that okay?"

"Yes. That's okay." They just continued walking in the darkness. The girls sighed. "Can I ask you something?"

"Yes."

"What would I do if you died? If you died, I would want to die. I wouldn't know what else to do. I would want to be with you."

"Be with me?"

"Yes. All the time. Forever."

"Okay. I promise I will be with you all the time, forever." He took her hand. "Pumpkin, do you still have the two kitchen knives?" She was about to answer, but he put his finger to her lips to silence her, just pointing to the black walls of the cottage. They were close now, and only a few trees hid them from the sight of somebody who might be there. "You stay here and wait until I get you."

The girl's pale face, framed by chocolate brown curls, looked scared and much older than her six years. It was the face of a girl who had lost her childhood and she had eyes that had seen things no little girl should see, eyes that looked too drawn and tired. She was born into chaos. A child mature beyond her years. Always moving, always on the run. She didn't know it any different, but she was not used to it yet. She had had toys, but had to leave them behind somewhere. They couldn't afford to carry a teddy bear or a toy car when her rucksack could be filled with food and drink. She was just six years old, and she was being asked to be ready to defend herself with a kitchen knife if need be.

"Hide, if you do not see me coming back but someone else and if they see you, just run. Ok? Use these knives if there's nothing else you can do."

"Dad," she said in her high voice, "Can't we stay together?" The man shook his head.

"Stay here. If I tell you to run, you run. Understand? If everything is ok, I will pick you up." The girl nodded.

"Be careful, daddy", she whispered, her big eyes looking even larger behind her glasses. He ruffled her hair.

"Don't worry; we'll be fine." He gave her a reassuring smile and walked towards the cottage. He could already see that there was not much left, but the walls were still standing, and there was even part of a roof. They would be dry for tonight. It was surprising, after so many chaotic weeks, coming this far. They had been lucky, always keeping away from open roads, just picking up leftovers like cans of coke or packets of sweets and crisps when such things were still available. He remembered how it had started a lifetime ago and only six years. It was Tuesday when the world burnt. Since then he had witnessed neighbours fighting neighbours. It had begun with looks, sarcastic comments about how people looked too much like terrorists, followed by stones being thrown, people being spat at and later knives, fire and bodies in the street being stepped over and ignored by ordinary people turned looters carrying bags full of stolen goods. Police tried to restore order, but there were too few, they could just watch, being powerless to stop any of it. And maybe, maybe they even agreed with some attacks. Well, at least in the beginning. It was the others who started this. Right. Not good Christians. No, Muslims. Or had they? Mad racism had oozed out of everyone, particularly in big cities like London, Paris and Munich, as people tried to get some justice or at least their version of the truth. Only fighting each other and everyone who didn't appear European enough, whatever that meant. And looters used the opportunity grabbing what they could take. Tuesday was the day when his city had panicked, spiralling out of control. It was a moment in time when the war took everyone with it, guilty or innocent and the government realised they couldn't get it under control. Tuesday wasn't the day when it was the most serious, but it was the day when the fuse was lit when buildings exploded, and they killed people on such a scale that the government installed martial law. To start with people expected the police to put everything back to how it should be and later, when they couldn't cope anymore everyone was expecting the forces but they were fighting in the middle east, Ireland, and other places. Anywhere but London. People didn't wait for the government. They took matters into their own hands.

Chapter 3

17th of September 2021 London Shepards Bush- Stanlake Road
Benazir

"Benazir!" Get up. We have to say our prayers. "Come on. Allah doesn't enjoy waiting for you. He's got better things to do. It's five o'clock."

"Coming." Thirteen-year-old Benazir yawned and stretched his arms above his head. His fingers smoothed back his thick black hair. The boy was a good-looking lad with friendly features and thick eyebrows complementing his light brown eyes. Not that he cared how he looked at this time of the day or any other time. His legs had twisted into a strange position while he had been asleep and he uncrossed them, smoothed his pyjamas and stood up as though about to leave. The boy spoke to the empty room with a sigh of tiredness and resignation. "Does it have to be that early?" He stared at the wall in front of him and sighed again. Sleep was slipping away. It would be a day like any other. The boy spread the little carpet out and kneeled down. He remembered his prayers by heart and needed no reminders:

"I seek refuge in Allah from Satan the outcast. Allah! There is none worthy of worship but He, the Ever-Living, the One Who sustains and protects all that exists.

Neither slumber nor sleep overtakes Him. To Him belongs whatever is in the heavens and whatever is on the earth. Who is he that can intercede with Him except with His permission?

He knows what happens to them in this world, and what will happen in the Hereafter. And they will encompass nothing of His knowledge except that which He wills. His throne extends over the heavens and the earth, and He feels no fatigue in guarding and preserving them. And He is the Highest, the Greatest."

Benazir appreciated he should say this in Arabic too, but he didn't speak the language and found it very hard to feel connected to prayers he didn't understand. When he spoke English, this prayer always made him feel like he could do anything. Allah was giving him the strength to achieve what he wanted, perhaps even get the red Nike Air Force trainers he had wanted for so long. It was possible. Benazir remembered when he had been sick for a very long time last year, Allah had helped him to get over it so he could continue serving him. His mum had just given him some medicine and told him he would get better soon. And his dad had taught him that nothing mattered other than Allah. As long as he worshiped him, followed the rules and made others follow the rules, everything would be ok. And it was fun. Benazir liked his religion. It made him feel loved, and it was fun meeting with all the other boys for prayers and days out. Only the getting up early bit bothered him. But he didn't mind following these rituals. And he realised what it meant for him. He had always wanted to help people by being an Iman. Ali, the one in his local Masjid Daar us Sunnah mosque was his big idol. He could always answer his questions, and he made everything fun. He had even found the time to play with him when he was younger. Benazir wanted to be like Ali. The boy smiled. "I will serve you, Allah", he said to the empty room. "You will look after me and my baby sister Aisha, mum and dad. Nothing bad will ever come upon us." His dad had told him Allah needed a lot more people who would want to serve him and spread the message and that it was going to take a while. But it shouldn't be a big deal, right? If people heard the message, they would want to serve Allah. They wouldn't hesitate. Everybody wanted to be saved. The boy bit his lips. Who was he kidding? It would be the hardest job ever. He was just thirteen years old. His dad had worked as Allah's servant his whole life, and there were still so many people who didn't listen to him. But Benazir knew of not being alone. He needed to do something about all the Muslims that suffered. All these children who would cry themselves to sleep all night. And doing it in these nice red Nike sneakers wouldn't do any harm. Benazir had watched a lot of television with his father, and his dad had showed him what these evil non-believers did every day. All those bombs in Islamic countries. Dozens and nobody stopped them. But he would. Allah would put an end to it. And Benazir could help him. His dad would tell him how. He needed someone to talk to, someone to make plans with. Exactly like his dad who had all these friends he met with twice a week. The boy smiled. He could ask his friend Ali. His best friend at school. Benazir's dad didn't allow him to be in the room when his dad and his friends started to whisper. But he and Ali had tried to sneak in and listen a couple of times. He couldn't talk to his mother about it. They didn't have the sort of relationship where you talked about problems. You just got on with things. But Benazir's father started to recognise him. He started to see him as a man and not as a child anymore. Benazir could see it in his eyes, the pride and a glowing fire of… something… something else he couldn't quite specify. He got up, rolled up his carpet and walked downstairs needing to talk to his father. "Mama" the boy cried. He was almost falling down the stairs trying to run faster than he could."Where's dad? I need to ask him to… I need to ask him something."

"He's not here", his mother snapped at him, when he arrived downstairs. He flinched at the aggressive tone of her voice. Although they didn't have a very warm relationship, he didn't feel he deserved such a reaction.

"I just need to talk to dad, please. It's important. I know what I want to do when I grow up." He could see her taking a deep breath.

"Sorry, Ben. I am tired, "she muttered and stared at him. She was waiting for him to say more. But he didn't. The boy didn't know how to explain to her what he felt. Yes, she was a religious woman, and she made sure he said his prayers, but how could he explain to her he wanted to be an Imam, explain that he wanted to preach. His dad would understand. He would be proud of him. But his mother would find out anyway, so perhaps it was better to get it over and done with.

"I suppose I better let you in on this."

"In on what?" she smiled. It was strange because she didn't smile often. Maybe the boy only imagined things, but his mother suddenly seemed interested in what he had to say. She was walking slower than normal and turning her head in his direction. He didn't know how his mother would react. He wasn't sure how religious she was. Everything she did, seemed about fulfilling her duties. She never appeared to care about anything. But if she didn't like it, he probably could squeeze out a few tears. Not that she was a woman who would feel sorry, but she would let him go to have lessons or whatever he needed, if his dad agreed. He needed to think. Could it be that his mother would be happy and finally love him? He didn't presume so, but he couldn't rule out the idea either. Maybe being an Imam would be so special it meant whatever had stopped her from loving him or showing her love would break that barrier. The boy just opened his mouth to tell her the great news, when she kicked shut the kitchen door, turned around to him and just said: "Maybe you should talk to your dad first. He is not home right now because he has important business to do. Benazir stopped moving altogether. He breathed quietly, trying to contain himself. His mind concentrated on the noises the fridge made. It sounded like it was breathing, snoring even. No, she didn't love him.

"When will he be back?" was all he whispered.

"Excuse me, but may I come in?" a man's voice behind Benazir pulled him out of his thoughts.

"Who are you and how did you get in?" Benazir's mother shrieked breathless, sounding angry and in control at the same time.

"It doesn't matter who I am. I just have a message from your husband. Everything worked according to the plan, and he will be home in an hour." He just turned around and left before Benazir, or his mother could say anything.

"Mum, who was that?"

"Quiet, just go in the kitchen and eat your breakfast. There is a glass of milk for you. Drink it. Don't give it to the cat." She was talking to Ben, but he could see his mother's mind was somewhere else. She didn't seem to be happy about the news that his father would be home soon. Or perhaps something else was bothering her. But the boy didn't dare to challenge his mother. She was not a woman to mess around with. And he wasn't in the mood for being slapped. He had disagreed once or twice with her and wished afterwards he hadn't. She was one of the few stay-at-home moms where they lived, and one time he had asked why she didn't work like all the other mums of the kids in his class. She just said that this was what Allah and his father wanted and he needed to accept that.

Benazir had just opened his mouth and a "but" had slipped out. Half a second later she had slapped his face. She said she expected him to accept the way they were and not question it because that's what good Muslims did. His mother had never been one to spare his feelings. Well, he would just sit here and wait.

Chapter 4

18th of September 2021 London Shepards Bush-Tunis Road
Mark

The screaming coming from outside drowned out all the words his dad could have said to comfort Mark. The boy just stood still when the first shot broke the living room window. It had covered the floor in a pile of broken glass, dirt and water that wind and rain were forcing in. His mother screamed.

"Are you ok Mark?" she yelled. The boy just screamed back:

"I am alright!" hating the tinny sound of fear being too obvious in his voice. He wanted to be strong. He wanted to be a man. But all he felt like was running back into the bedroom and hide under his Batman covers. His mother came racing into the room and screamed again. But now it wasn't a scream of surprise. It was true horror. And this was when Mark turned around and realised the bullet had hit his dad's head. His mum was already on her knees, stroking her husband's face, screaming at him to wake up, kissing him, and moving the dark brown hair that covered his eyes, sobbing. Mark needed to be a grown-up now. He had to take control of the situation. And the most logical thing was to call an ambulance. Maybe his dad was just unconscious. Yes, that's it. Only unconscious. He ran to the phone in the hallway and dialled 999. But the line was dead. Mobile phone. Don't panic. Use your mobile phone. 999. Again nothing. It didn't work. What was happening here? He remembered he had just taken out his sim card yesterday to change it. He needed to call 112. His hands were shaking when he dialled. He could still hear his mum sobbing in the living room. She knew. But Mark didn't want to accept it. Finally, he got through to an operator, and they told him they would be there as soon as they could. The woman sounded stressed, but perhaps it was just Mark's imagination. All he could do now was to go back to his mum, his dad and wait. He was dreading it. But he was in charge now. Mark forced his feet to move and looked around the room. It was still messy, and his mum was still on the floor, holding his dad's body tight as if she could bring him back to life. To stand there, watching his mother falling apart felt like hours, but in reality, it couldn't have been over thirty minutes until the ambulance and the police arrived. When the doorbell rang, Mark felt a wave of relief sweeping over him. Somehow it ripped his mum out of her lethargy. She almost ran to the door and opened it with both hands as if it took all her strength. When she saw the tall, dark-haired paramedic, she calmed down. She studied him as he spoke.

"Sally Mitchell? Your son Mark called us. He told us your name. Can we come in?"

"Yes, yes. Sure. This way, please. She gestured towards the living room. My husband is in there. A bullet hit his head. Someone shot through the window. I don't know why."

"People are crazy tonight. Some riots are going on out there. But the police are trying to get everything under control. May we please come in and take care of your husband?"

Mark who had just followed them in silence and watched the paramedic when he attended to his dad. His expression said it all. There was nothing this man could do. He just locked eyes with his fair-haired skinny colleague, who had walked in after him and shook his head.

"I am sorry Mrs Mitchell. I… there is… there's nothing we can do. He's… your husband has… he has left us." One second and nothing happened. Finally, she turned around and glared at him.

"What the hell are you talking about? You are nothing more than a… a… a… What kind of paramedic are you, anyway? Nothing but a nurse. Nothing."

"Mum, please." She silenced Mark with an abrupt gesture.

"Ma'am, I know you are angry and upset. I understand that. We will take your husband to the hospital, and you and your son can come with us. But it won't bring him back. I'm sorry." Marks' mother looked at the man with a mad expression in her eyes.

"You're one of them, right? I can see that. Your dark hair and the colour of your skin. You're one of those. These people who started all this. These people who shot Milo. It's your fault. All of this is your fault." She was now screaming at the top of her lungs.

"Mum, Mum. Calm down. The doctor is just trying to help." Mark pulled his mother's hand, but she just shook it off.

"He's not helping, and he's not a doctor. If he were a doctor, your dad would be alive."

The paramedic frowned, but reacted professionally. Probably had heard abuse like that before.

"Mam, the police will bring in a team who need to go over every detail. I know this is difficult, but they will have to find out what happened. They need to have a clear picture of what went on. I will leave you alone with your husband and your son for a minute. The police are waiting outside."

"Sons."

"Pardon?"

"Sons. Mark has a brother. Brian. He is upstairs, sleeping."

"Ok, mam. You will stay here, and I will make sure Brian is ok." The dark-haired paramedic got up, leaving them with his colleague and walked towards the light wooden stairs leading to the first floor.

"No. You. Will. Not. You will stay right where you are." Sally's voice sounded ice cold. Nobody had seen her getting the gun she was now pointing at the paramedic. Mark didn't even know they had a gun in the house. "My husband might be dead, but you aren't getting my son. Milo will be the last victim you kill."

"Mrs Mitchell, plea…" She hit him in the thigh stopping the words escaping from his lips. There was a lot of blood. She must have hit the paramedic's artery just right. Before she could do any more, two policemen, who had been waiting outside, kicked in the door. They had no choice but to shoot her.

Nobody saw Brian coming downstairs, still sleepy, not knowing what was going on, and running straight into his mother's arms covering her body when the bullet went flying in her direction. He collapsed. His mother, looking all red and splotchy, just stood there. Mark was racing towards them, but his feet felt like being glued to the floor. He couldn't get to them quick enough. One policeman was attending to the injured paramedic, and the other one caught Mark. He kicked and yelled trying to free himself. But he was too weak. He wasn't a man yet. He was only thirteen years old. A very young and small thirteen-year-old boy. He just gave up and hung in the arms of the policeman who was leading him outside. They just stood there for a minute, and Mark stared at the floor. Was this a nightmare? This couldn't be happening. Somehow there was some vain hope in his mind. Hope that somehow, they would all be okay. He wanted his mum. But she was still inside. He could hear her kicking, screaming and sobbing. What did they do to his brother and father? What had they done with their bodies? It didn't occur to him to ask the copper who was steering Mark to his police vehicle. All he noticed was that everything looked different outside. His life was a big, stupid nightmare and he would never wake up. The boy was bending his head to get into the car when he heard a noise. A metallic clacking followed by something he couldn't identify until his mind started to work again. Mark had heard that sound before. He had heard it on television. The clicking of a gun which was being unlocked. His head turned. His eyes darted to where the noise had come from, trying to adjust to the dark. The policeman let go of him. Mark stepped back. The dim street lights were shining right at the spot where they were standing.

"You should let that boy leave. He won't go with you" the deep voice of a teenager snarled.

The policeman just took a deep breath, trying to remain calm.

"I'm not forcing him to come. His mother is injured, and they'll all need help. My colleague over there is just tending to a paramedic who got injured in the house. We need to go. We're doing our job and we're only here so nobody else will die."

For a moment Mark caught sight of the teenager's face. He was holding a gun to the policeman's head. Beneath the navy-blue baseball cap, he was wearing, Mark saw the pale, freckled face of a boy who was no older than fifteen, twisted into a rictus mask of anger, almost hate. In a blur of movement, the policeman tried to twist his body, pull out his gun and push the teenager away. But he forgot about Mark standing too close. He stumbled over him, and the shot went past its intended aim. It happened too quick to remember anything more than the policeman collapsing and the teenager sniggering.

"You can go now, boy. He won't take you."

The sniggerer had used his gun when he had the chance. A dark patch of crimson was spreading out across the policeman's back. Mark turned and ran back into the house but left the door open. Big mistake. The teenager followed him.

"Where're you going, mate? Don't run. You need not be afraid. The police aren't coming. Tonight, we're free."

What the hell was this guy talking about? All Mark wanted was to make sure his mother was ok. That was the only reason he went back to his house. The bodies of his brother and father would still be there. He was sure about that. He paid no more attention to the teenager following him. Why weren't there more people? His mother had shot a paramedic. His brother was dead. The house should buzz with people. Where was the other doctor? Mark collapsed onto the floor of the house crying out for his mother, whimpering. No, he wouldn't lose it. He needed to be strong. His thoughts went to their neighbours. They weren't close to any of them but why hadn't they come to see what was going on? Maybe the world had gone crazy, and they were all dead or had fled already, not caring about Mark and his mum. He didn't want to hear it.

Chapter 5

Ross-on-Wye, Herefordshire

Five years later

But all that mattered was they were here now, and for tonight they would be safe. He let go of the little girl's hand. They both realised they could not stand here forever. She cowered behind a bush and watched him walk away. Ducking and running, trying to make as little noise as possible. He turned around a couple of times keeping his gun to hand in his pocket, touching the cold metal as if it could reassure him everything would be ok. When he reached the cottage, he could smell its burned walls. There was no sign of life. He stayed within the shadows of its ruins and moved forward. His feet left prints in the ash covering everything. There was a leathery corpse leaning against the side. The man almost fell over it. But it didn't scare him. He had seen too many already. He just grimaced and cursed. A wave of relief washed over his body when he entered the house. People had abandoned the place a long time ago. Nobody would hide upstairs. There was no upstairs, and the house had no cellar either. He had another glimpse. The empty table with extra plates and cups had seen better times. Some broken chairs scattered around the room were witnesses of some scumbags who had once been here. The man sighed and plodded back to where the little girl had been waiting for him.

He ducked. Something was wrong. There was danger in the air. Rancid and foul. His feet shuffled around. Quiet.

An old man with a gone-out cigarette between his teeth and a drool slowly running down his chin had grabbed the little girl with one hand. He spat out and pulled the girl closer. "Got something to eat?" he whispered. She said nothing, just holding the kitchen knife in her little hand being too scared to use it.

"Can't you talk? Well, I guess being on your own you forget things like that. Who can you talk to anyway, being all on your own? It's surprising you have survived that long. You need someone to take care of you. Consider it. I mean I would do it. I do you a favour. You do me a favour. How does that sound?"

He bent down trying to kiss the girl. The girl's father crept up on the old guy. He was too busy trying to rub himself on the little girl to notice what was happening behind him. But the girl saw her dad. She recognised she would be alright. There was a lake just behind the cottage. She could see it from here. This meant they could collect firewood tonight and wash themselves tomorrow morning. All she needed to do was use the knife and give her father time to fight. She looked up at the oak trees being lined up everywhere as if to bear witness to what was going on here. She could hear the birds singing and felt the old man's drool running down her chin. Some trees had long ago been cut down, but nobody had chopped them and picked up the wood. She jumped forward and pushed the knife into the old man's right thigh.

"Arggggh. You stupid bitch."

The old man collapsed on one knee, letting go of the little girl. He was injured but not hurt enough for her to be able to run. Before she could get away, he grabbed her again. Brown leaves. She could see lots of brown leaves on the ground before the old man's fist punched her in the face. The last thing the girl remembered was her father pulling out his knife and plunging it into the old man's back. The bullets in his gun were too valuable to be used if there were other means of defence. Assurance washed over her she would be ok before she lost consciousness.

The first thing she saw, when she came by, was her father's face looking at her, smiling. She was lying on a bed. The mattress was mouldy, and it stank, but it was a real bed. "Hi, pumpkin. Are you okay?" He kept touching her face.

"Listen, I am so sorry for leaving you there. We should have walked together. I shouldn't have asked you to stay behind. I promise I will never do that again."

"Dad?"

"Yes?"

"It's ok. I am still here, and you're still here." She pushed herself up, resting her face in her hand. It burned like fire coiling around her skin, but she didn't want her dad to know. "Are we in the cottage?"

"Well, what's left of it. Yes."

"You've made a fire. You shouldn't do that. It's dangerous."

"I know, but our clothes are still wet. They need to dry. We cannot afford to be ill." She saw that he was barefoot and had rolled his trousers up to his knees. "Dad, where are your shoes?"

"Don't worry, pumpkin. They're drying by the fire. Everything's fine."

"Dad?"

"What is it?"

"Why do you always call me pumpkin? It's something to eat, isn't it? Are you hungry?"

The man laughed out loud. "I'm always hungry. But that's not why I call you pumpkin. A pumpkin is a sweet vegetable but not too sweet. Exactly right… like you, darling." He smiles and takes her hand. She frowns.

"Where's the man?"

"He's gone."

"Oh, ok. He was bad."

"I know."

It was still the middle of the night. She couldn't have been asleep for long. Her ears strained but all she could hear was the crackling of the fire and the periodic hooting of an owl. It made her feel peaceful.

The cottage had no glass windows left, but her father had covered the holes with wood planks. They wouldn't hide the light from the fire. But it didn't matter. She felt warm, cosy and safe, even though she was aware it was an illusion.

They both had stopped speaking and were just listening to whatever their mind focused on. It was a perfect moment of her childhood. A childhood that was long gone. It should be like this every night. To feel protected and warm in their own home. But they both realised it wouldn't last. The cold would come back, and her dad was growing colder. This life made them both age quicker. There would be a day when she would have to fend for herself.

Something had burned the country down, the ashened shapes of humanity's remains stood out as a reminder of the old times, and the little flocks of something were snowing down on everybody wherever they went. It looked like snow, but it was ash raining down. The ash of everything that had burned–waste, buildings, trees, animals, people. "We need to eat," the man said. "I caught a rabbit."

"I didn't know there were any rabbits left."

"Yes, there are. Few. But they breed quick. It's on the fire. I found an old pot and matches. I'm cooking it properly. There's water in a little stream behind the house."

"Someone could smell it."

"I know. But we have to eat."

"We could have eaten it raw."

"We could have. But sometimes I'm so tired of only surviving."

The girl just looked at him. She never learned another life. Her father had told her about the old days. When food was being bought in shops and people felt warm just by pushing a button. It sounded like a fairy tale. How could it be possible?

"I even found some colour pencils. They still work. There is no paper, but you can draw on the walls."

"What are colour pencils?"

"Here, I will show you. That's what you do with them?" He drew a little yellow flower on the wall behind her. All she could think of was using the black and red pencils to draw fire and ash, painting the long nights they had seen so many times, feeling cold and being scared. But she couldn't draw that. It wasn't possible. She just took the green pencil her dad gave her and painted some grass. It didn't seem to be real, but it was fun. A sun followed and a house that wasn't burning, followed by a picture of her father. This made him smile. It looked nothing like him, but he loved it. She had never seen him smile. It made her feel better. It made her feel as if from now on things would improve. He held the girl who wasn't cold anymore and kissed her head. It was nothing like the drooling kiss the old man had given her. Her dad's embrace made her feel like she wanted to put her arms around him, just staying there forever. But the rabbit was ready, and he got up to get it. The odour was beautiful, better than anything she could remember. And the taste. It was like the meat was melting in her mouth. He pulled the cover around them, and they just sat in this old bed eating their rabbit stew. When the girl had finished, she looked up and saw he had fallen asleep. She listened to the distant sound of thunder and sat up straight. She lay awake a long time just listening. Tonight, they wouldn't get wet. They had a fire to stay dry by. Getting wet wasn't a good thing. You could catch a cold which could turn into something worse and they could die. This is how it would be for a long time, she realised with a growing sense of dread, running away from dangerous people scavenging for leftover food. Maybe they should stop pretending that things would get back to normal one day. Whatever that normal was. Streets full of life, full of people, friendly people. Shops with food you could just buy. Not having to worry about people who wanted to hurt you. She had seen the remains of this old world. Moulded letters were hanging on building walls that were half collapsing. Signs above looted stores, broken shop windows, weeds growing on old carpets. But for her, it had never been real. She had just been born when everything collapsed. She couldn't remember it being any different. But it was nice listening to all these stories. For her, it was just fairy tales. Fairy tales that now and then pushed through to the real world. Her mum, dad and brother used to live in London. She knew of that but couldn't remember any of it. Her mother had died when she was still a baby, and her brother had disappeared after that. She couldn't remember him or her mother, but she remembered how the streets used to sound. They sounded of fear. She tucked a dark lock behind one ear. She recalled the running. They were always running from something or someone. Her father had taken care of her. She was always scared, but she could rely on him. Yes, she recollected the sense of trust, even though she could not have been older than two or three. To start with there were always police cars and fire engines. But soon that had stopped. The gunshots hadn't. Memories from her younger mind flickered into her consciousness. She remembered so little from London. She had only been a toddler, and her father had carried her everywhere. Sometimes people had helped them. Mostly women. That was nothing she remembered. It was only something her daddy had told her. There was always chaos. It filled her whole life with turmoil and confusion. Never knowing what was to come. Always hurrying to find some food and being eager to get to some place they could call home for a moment and just lock the door. People smashing windows and running away was part of daily life.

She just sat there in silence listening to the quiet snoring of her dad, not missing anything. Well, at least she thought she didn't. She pursed her lips considering it. The only thing she yearned for, even though she couldn't remember, was her mother. Yes, she missed her mum. Her face creased with concentration. If they could bring her mother back somehow, that would be good.

At night time. Yes, at night time she missed her the most, when she was awake, and her dad had fallen into a twitching sleep from exhaustion. She smiled at an imagined memory. Yes, sometimes she needed a reason to smile even if it was just for a phantasy.

Chapter 6

18th of September 2021 London Shepards Bush- Stanlake Road
Benazir

At 2 o'clock in the morning he was still waiting. Breakfast had come and gone. He had spent hours in school, walked home and done his homework.

His father wouldn't come back and his mother said nothing, just doing her duties. Like a good housewife and mother. There was no passion. She just did what her parents had taught her. But she didn't talk to him, just wiping the kitchen tops again and again. Benazir had gone to bed at about ten o'clock after doing his leftover maths homework. But he couldn't sleep. His window was open, and at some point, the boy could hear something that sounded like shooting. He listened to it in the dark, straining his eyes and thought he saw some flashes. It seemed too loud and close. Where did the shooting sound come from? Maybe it was as near as the newspaper agent at the end of his road. Where was his dad? What had happened? He felt thirsty, and tonight he wouldn't get any sleep before his dad came home. There was no point staying in bed. The shooting had stopped. There was a pause. Yes, he would make people talk to each other when he was old enough. He would make sure there were no guns.

There were voices outside. His mother was on the phone: "Tell me where you are and I will pick you up. I will wait for you to come out. Nobody will know. I know this has nothing to do with me. But I am still your wife. I will support you with whatever you do."

Who was she talking to?

"Mum, was that dad? When is he coming home?" Sirens. Her head jerked up.

"Why aren't you in bed? It's late. You know you have to get up at sunrise to say your prayers."

Benazir looked at the window. It was pitch black outside apart from the dim streetlights. But he could see something unusual in the distance. The sky had turned orange, dipping the horizon into a glowing brilliance, like the burn of a fire, as if the sun had decided it didn't want to go to bed tonight, staying and waiting around for dawn.

"Mum. Why don't you tell me where dad is? That man said he would be back in an hour. That was ages ago."

Across the street, he could hear people shouting, but they lived in a noisy neighbourhood. He recognised the voices, but they didn't worry him. He heard someone parking his car in front of their house. But he was used to people coming and going all night long, be it at the neighbours or further down the road.

"Mum?" She just looked at him. He could see she was just about to tell him something when his baby sister Aisha started crying. Why now? Someone had lit a fire outside. What was going on here tonight? He turned around to ask his mum again, but she had gone upstairs to check on Aisha. He just followed her. The tree in front of his sister's bedroom window shaded the whole room. It was night, but even during the day it always created a strange shadowy effect and gave the walls a rich pattern. He never liked it, but his sister didn't mind. She was just a baby.

Maybe dad has died. Why did he presume that? His parents' relationship, their marriage always seemed kind of strange to him. He never expected them to love each other. But he was aware it had been an arranged marriage. I meant it to be. His parents would find a bride for him one day when he was old enough unless he became an Imam and didn't marry. But today was weird, almost like a dream, a strange twilight with his dad not being here and his mum not talking to him. He could see her standing in his sister's room holding the baby in her arms trying to calm her. She turned around to Benazir when she heard him. There was a grave expression on her face. He'd seen it.

She was hiding something. It was the same look she had on her face when she found out that Benazir had been in a church. She hadn't told him that she knew. But he could see the disappointment and his dad had given him a good hiding when he had come home later that day. The boy reached out with one hand and stepped closer. His sister had stopped crying but his mother stepped back so he couldn't touch her. Benazir just stood there, sensing her breath on his face, the muscles of which started to flex. His chest felt tight. All he wanted to do was to put his arms around his mother, but he was sure she wouldn't let him.

"Where is he, mum? Tell me. Is he coming back?"

Living in this family, Benazir accepted that life was unpredictable, and so was his father. Sometimes he was loving, and sometimes he just shouted at him, losing himself in his temper to the point of being violent. At least his mother was predictable. She showed no love, but there was never any surprise in her behaviour either. She was almost like a robot doing her duties. He wanted to please his dad, but he had a soft spot for his mother even though he was aware she didn't return his love. She just did what she had to do and dealt with anything life tossed her way.

"No, I don't think so."

"What?" A cold stream of air ran down his back.

"Your dad. I don't think he will come back tonight. Or ever."

"Where is he?"

"He's doing what Allah told him to do."

"What Allah told him to do? What does that mean?"

"You will see. The world will change soon." The shootings had started again. "You should go back to bed."

"What are you talking about? Mum?"

He was shouting at her now, disrespecting his mother, but he couldn't help himself. Her hands were shaking. She would drop his sister if she wasn't careful.

"Mum? Don't you want to sit down? Give me Aisha. Please."

His mother didn't protest when he took the baby from her. And he had just covered his sister with her blanket when the first shot hit his mother in the back. The bullet had come out on the other side, and the small patch of blood on her tummy grew bigger by the second. Benazir studied her face, waiting for her to say something. When she collapsed, he just looked down and moved off to the side. Aisha needed his help. The voices outside grew louder. He needed to move his baby sister away from the window. Where could he go? The bathroom. Yes, the bathroom was the safest place in the house. It didn't have a window, just an extraction fan. The second bullet bounced off the metal frame of Aisha's bed. It would have killed her. The gunshot was too loud. It didn't sound real. But Benazir didn't care. He just started running. The bathroom. Yes, he would be safe in the bathroom, and when his dad came home, he would take care of everything. Before he left the room, his head turned around, and he could see a group of bald guys standing outside. They were laughing. Benazir didn't think they saw him. His mum hadn't turned the lights on. She had just been unlucky to stand right by the window. The room didn't have curtains. They didn't have to be good shooters. An easy kill with the first cold shot. They had worked fast. But why? Benazir didn't have time to think about the why. Three shots followed. They wanted to make sure everybody in the house was dead. The laughing and sniggering went right through his stomach. *Run.* Aisha was awake, but she didn't cry. If he were lucky, she wouldn't start. She was a quiet baby and probably just surprised by everything that was going on. She didn't react as if she was in danger. Another shot. Benazir continued running downstairs, he almost fell and didn't stop until he reached the bathroom and had locked the door. Panic. He was panicking. He had seen six people standing outside. All with shaved heads. Why were they there? This was a Muslim neighbourhood. These people didn't belong here. He leaned against the bath and started praying.

"I know you are here and see my tears. I know you hear my prayers and you are testing me. And all I ask from you is strength so I can handle this struggle, what I am facing right now and that I have patience. I love you, my Lord. My Allah. Please keep me safe. Ameen."

Loud screams outside. He could hear the panic in the screamer's voice. And then… the gunshots again, the laughing and… silence.

Someone was knocking on the door. It almost sounded as if the person was trying to kick in the door. These people were too close. If they came in, he wouldn't be safe in the bathroom.

"Please, Aisha, don't cry. Not now." Benazir begged silently. He ducked lower, not that he could hide much in the small room, shuffled backwards as much as he could, still clinging on to his baby sister. He could almost detect burned gunpowder, but that was just imagination. People had screamed again, and the voices were ringing in his ears. *Don't worry*, he told himself. It will soon be over. He felt sick, his heart was beating in his ears, and his hands were shaking, but he had to take care of his sister. His mother was dead and his father… was not home yet. He needed to decide. Stay here and wait for his dad who might never come. Try to get out through the back door and risk being seen or worse, Aisha drawing attention. He sat still for a moment and listened to the screaming. The kicking had stopped, but he couldn't stay here. He laid his sister down on the floor and stood up. Slowly he opened the bathroom door with one hand. Nobody. He looked down. His sister was asleep. He picked her up, stepped out and walked the same way he had come in. Before Benazir reached the step leading upstairs, he turned to the left walking through the kitchen to the back door. They locked the rear door, but he also knew where his mum kept the keys. He trudged to the kitchen drawer knowing he would find what he was looking for. His mother had left the television on, but she had turned down the volume. His eyes scanned past the screen. The news was on. Some special report. He wasn't interested and would have walked right past it if they wouldn't have shown the picture of a man that looked familiar to him. The boy's head jerked back, and he looked again. The man on the screen, the man, the reporter was talking about was his dad. He took a sharp breath in. No doubt. It was his father. But this couldn't be. Why was he on television? Benazir was desperate to find out what had happened but he couldn't turn up the volume without drawing attention. Or could he? The shooting, laughing and screaming hadn't stopped. There were breaks in between the noises, but there was never complete silence. A hunt was going on outside. The boy had no idea who was being hunted exactly, but he had a good guess. His fellow neighbours. All of them Muslims. Things

had escalated. The usual racist comments and snide remarks had turned into something much worse.

An explosion. On the screen. He put Aisha on the kitchen table and turned up the volume slightly, just enough for him to hear what the reporter was saying. He didn't know the guy who was speaking. He had never been interested in politics. The news reporter looked sick and badly shaken, but he was professional enough to know an opportunity when he saw one. His words were purely instinctive. They almost sounded banal. But they weren't. It was a massacre. An Islamic terrorist attack on the Eiffel Tower, Big Ben and the Oktoberfest. There was no better word to describe it but slaying. The perfect word for what had been going on. But there was one big difference between all three locations. Londoners had attacked Big Ben. Londoners who had been living there for years. And they could identify two of them. Tarek Al-Kashir and Ali El-Tanek. Benazir's father. He even recognised the first person. Not his name, Tarek. But he remembered him. It was the same man who had told his mum that dad would be home soon. And according to the reporter, he was on the run. His father wasn't. His father wouldn't come back. Not today or any other day. He died when he decided to be a suicide bomber taking many people with him when detonating a bomb near Big Ben.

Benazir was on his own. He was only thirteen years old, but he understood what was happening. He realised why these people had been trying to kick in the door. Why they had shot a lot of people outside. These bold guys had found out that one of the suicide bombers lived in this street. They just hadn't figured out yet which house it was exactly. Benazir needed to run. If he wanted to live, he needed to get out now. He couldn't wait for the police. They would come they might come too late. For one second he considered taking his iPad, but what was that good for now? He grabbed his baby sister and settled her into his left arm. His right hand was free. It was shaking when he unlocked the dead bolts but he managed. The shooting and screaming sounded muffled. There was no-one here, but it wouldn't take long until they figured that there was another way out. And… that someone was still in the house. Someone who wasn't dead yet. It was just a matter of time until Aisha started crying. Aisha? He couldn't leave like that. Where would he go? And even if he could think of someone. He needed food and drinks, baby formula. Bang. The kicking had started again. Laughter. A man laughing. To the boy it sounded like the devil. If there was such a thing. Something evil was trying to get in and there was nobody here who could help him. Nobody. Not even his father. A man he had looked up to. Benazir had wanted to follow in his footsteps. Someone who was so religious he had been an inspiration to Benazir. And yes, he presumed if everybody would be Muslim the world would be a better place. But killing innocent people to achieve that? No, that was wrong. Innocent people should not be killed. The bible allowed you to defend yourself. But detonating bombs at all these places was not a defence; it was pure murder. *Bang. Bang. Bang.* The massive oak front door was strong but it wouldn't hold forever. Benazir picked up his school rucksack which he had tossed carelessly on the floor. His school books scattered around the floor. He didn't care about it. Aimlessly he threw some sweets, bread and baby formula in. He almost forgot that he needed drinks too. Water. There were always bottles of water in the cupboard. After he finished, he put the rucksack on his back, picked up his baby sister, wrapped her tightly in her blanket, stepped over the doorstep and shut the door as quietly as he could. Darkness surrounded him for a moment. Some streetlights had gone out. Bulbs that had burned out or had been broken by someone. Who knew? Today was crazy anyway. But things would be better soon. Or at least that that was what the boy hoped for. The question was who should he go to? He couldn't go to any of his family or friends here in the street. There was no guarantee they were alive or wouldn't have the same problem soon after he arrived. Maybe they wouldn't even let him in considering what his dad had done. If he had done anything. Perhaps they got it wrong. You always heard about these cases of mistaken identity. But deep-down Benazir realised his father was involved. It all made sense. All these nights when strange men were sitting in the living room and him and his mother hadn't been allowed to go in there. The day when his dad had told him all these people who died through the hand of suicide bombers somewhere in the world deserved what they'd got. He thought about his mum and how she was lying on her own in his sister's room. A small bang of guilt hit his heart but he couldn't feel any love. It was his duty to love her. She was a good mum. She did exactly what her parents told her and later her husband. But for some strange reason he couldn't feel anything right now. All he cared about was his baby sister Aisha.

Chapter 7

18th of September 2021 London Shepards Bush
Mark

"Mate. Please, mate. You will be alright. I know it's these damn lunatics. They started it all. Who would have thought it took so long for people to finally see it? But we'll fight back. Right? Yeah. We'll fight back."

What was this guy talking about? Mark turned his head looking at the teenager. His face was blotchy and still wet with tears.

"What lunatics? What are you on about? My dad's here. Someone shot him… my mum… my mum. How…how can I get to school tomorrow?" He started sobbing again.

"School's over mate. Sad. I know. I know. But it's these fucking bastards. Blew up Big Ben, killed many people. I hear what you're saying, bro. Your dad was a victim, but we'll find the bastards who've done this." The boy sniggered. "I mean did you see what I was doing to this bloody musulman out there? And that's just the beginning. Nobody will bully me now. School is oooout."

"What?"

All Mark could concentrate on was the familiarity of his Solo2 Headphones around his neck. He couldn't remember why he was still wearing them. And he was still too dazed to understand what the guy was mumbling. It had something to do with what he had seen on television, even though it seemed to be a lifetime ago. However, he couldn't quite make the connection. The teenage boy was now hopping from one foot to another as if he needed to go to the toilet.

"Come on. You were there. That cop, that Muslim bastard… pretending to be a police officer. Idiot. I showed him… yeah, I showed him where he belongs, blew his head off. Police. Hah. He probably just tried to smuggle a bomb somewhere or something like that. But you've got me now. You've got me to protect yeah… Oh, sorry I am T.J. I hunt on my own."

He held out his hand to Mark who was still on the floor. Mark looked at him. T.J. looked familiar. A frown appeared on Mark's forehead. Where did he know him from? And then he realised. T.J. was a boy one year above him. His entire class had bullied him and he always seemed to get into trouble. Mark didn't know him well but one thing was for sure, this guy didn't have many friends. Unless some peers had suddenly accepted him as their new mate, nobody would come and support him. But he was still holding a gun. And perhaps it was best if Mark pretended, he didn't recognise him. T.J. wasn't pointing the weapon at him but how could he know that guy wouldn't use it again? He had just killed a police officer and didn't seem the least bit worried about it or about the fact that the house would swarm with officers soon. But maybe he wasn't in danger. Not from this boy, anyway. Mark wasn't a Muslim. His mother wasn't a Muslim. His brother and father weren't Muslims either. Not that it mattered because they were both dead. But being in the house with a crazy racist guy and his gun who wanted to hunt everyone who followed Islam made it more comforting to seem properly European with light brown hair and blue eyes. Not that Mark had ever worried about his looks. But this minute it seemed to be important. He wondered if the paramedic had saved his colleague. "My mum's still in there, I think. We need to make sure she's ok. And there were two doctors. I mean paramedics. A gunshot injured one of them." The teenager didn't need to know it was his mother who had shot him. But what happened to the second police officer? Where was he?

"Ok, let's find your mum. I guess if there are two doctors in there, she'll be fine." T.J. hadn't listened to Mark. They both walked into the living room. The second policeman was holding his gun towards Mark's mum who was still cradling his brother Brian. Nothing had changed apart from the fact that she was not screaming anymore. Her screams had turned into quiet sobs. She looked up and smiled warmly at Mark. The paramedic was still trying to stop his bleeds. Judging from the amount of blood, he had probably injured an artery.

"What the...?" T.J. shouted. He fired twice. One bullet hit the surprised police officer. The other one killed the paramedic who would probably have died, anyway. "He was a Muslim," T.J. stated matter of fact, frowning as if he was trying to work out a complicated mathematical formula.

"I know. Thank you." Mark's mum answered. She was still sitting on the floor, now frowning at T.J., Mark just stood there looking at the second paramedic for help. But the guy just stared into thin air. He wouldn't do anything. Mark remembered watching a movie once where a girl ended up in another dimension. Everything looked the same, but things were different. Slightly. Colours were not as bright, and the voices of people sounded slightly muffled. They all acted like robots, and that was how Mark felt. This wasn't his house. It wasn't his birth mother and his real brother lying there on the floor. His birth mother would never have been capable of such hatred. She had liked his friends no matter what background they've had. Ok, she was never a saint, she'd made some cringe-worthy jokes before and always moaned about too many immigrants coming to her country. That's why she voted for the Brexit years ago but she would never have been able to kill a human being, no matter what religion he or she had. And she would never have said: "Thank you" to someone who just killed a policeman. Perhaps these people were terrible. But Mark remembered Muslims in his class, and they were alright. Mark liked one of them enough to become friends. A very religious boy who never bothered Mark and his mum had always welcomed him. This whole thing was so confusing. But his mum was still his mum. He needed to make sure she was alright.

T.J., now sitting on the floor, had taken Mark's mother's hand and was patting it.

When she spoke, he could hear the respect and yes, almost like in her tone of voice. It broke his heart. "You understand what's going on. The news. I mean they're here to get us." She turned to Mark. Her eyes were black with madness. "Mark, Darling. This lad's good. He knows what we are up against.

We need to stay with him. We need to get on with business. There're a lot more of them outside. And they're all here to destroy us. They want to kill us. Aren't they?" She looked at the frozen paramedic.

"That's right." T.J. nodded. They call it the Jihad and kill everybody who isn't one of them. But *he* looks useless." He waived the gun at the paramedic and smiled at him. "But you're not one of them. Make sure they don't kill you. We don't need you here. It's too late for us. Try to save some life somewhere else, will you?" The medic just stared at him. "Go," Mark shouted and the man ran for his life.

Mark moved and was now standing by the stairs next to the dead policeman and the equally dead paramedic. He nodded and pretended to agree with these two crazy people. "How many of them are here? I mean you cannot kill them all. Isn't it better to talk… to convince them?"

T.J. and his mum laughed out loud. The sound was bitter and full of hysteria. "Convince them?" they both said at the same time. They won't listen. It's them or us. You decide."

"Ok." Mark's voice was shaking. "Mum. These people… aren't they like us? I mean they have kids like you. Can't we just wait until all of this is over. The police, soldiers… I don't know. The government, they will help."

"My kids are dead… I mean… one… I mean Brian is dead. Nobody will help." She started sobbing again, almost crawling on the floor, her arms stretched in his direction. "I don't want to lose you. They'll kill you." T.J. looked at them motionless. "Your mother is right. Kill is what they do. They don't talk. No. And if they talk, it's just this stupid Arabic. They don't understand us. The only thing they understand is for us to fight back. Yeah. So, decide, boy. Will you fight with us?" He was shouting now. "Will you fight with us?" he repeated. Mark held on to the bloodstained bannister. "Ok. But they speak English, the ones I know. My fr…"

"What?"

"Ok."

"Say it louder."

"Ok, I'll fight back," Mark screamed at the top of his lungs. T.J. started laughing, and Mark's mum started sobbing still cradling Brian. Mark didn't join in the laughter. He just took a deep, shaky breath. "How are we going to start? I mean the police will be here soon."

"No, they won't, darling. You still do not understand what's going on outside tonight." His mum almost whispered. "It's the end of the world. Everybody has gone insane."

"But the police will come soon. And if they can't the army will come."

She smiled at him sadly, touching his arm. "There aren't enough of them. It's everywhere. The entire world. Puff." She raised her arms up. Mark gaped at her with his mouth wide open. He took a deep breath, trying to say something. Something about the government not letting this happen.

Scratching. What was it? There was a knock on the door. A weak, scared beat. It sounded almost as if someone wasn't sure if it was the right house.

Ross-on-Wye, Herefordshire
Five years later

The morning came far too quickly. They both had dreamed something pleasant and unrealistic, and both of them wished they could have stayed there. "It's raining," the girl said, propping her head on one hand, looking through a hole in the wooden panel covering the window. A few raindrops had landed on the ground, and she watched them turning into a little puddle. They would have to go out there soon. But could wait until the rain had stopped. She knew what her dad would say when she asked him. They shouldn't stay in one place for too long. But they had to find a place to settle, eventually. This wasn't it. He had never said this to her, but she had always assumed they couldn't stay on the road forever. They would become sick one day. Her dad was skilled in dressing wounds, healing them and he knew a lot about infections and other stuff. She had seen him looking at these big books he was carrying around with him. He studied them whenever they had the time. She wasn't a good reader. Her dad had tried to teach her, and she tried to do it on her own, but it was difficult. They were always on the move, always hungry and tired. There never seemed to be enough time to study anything, especially not learning how to read. Her dad didn't like it. He kept telling her she needed to learn how to take care of herself. She would need to read these books and study them herself, but they were just so big and had fancy titles like 'Herbal medicine' or 'First Aid and more'. They almost seemed like magical fairy tale books to her.

"We cannot stay. You know that." She hadn't heard her dad coming into the room again. He just stood there and looked at her with his sad, tired eyes. Even a night of good sleep couldn't wipe away the lines around his eyes. "I know", she replied and got up. "But it would be nice."

After they had packed everything, they just kept on walking in the desolate forest. After a few hours, they rested, had some dry bread, water from a stream and kept going. None of them spoke much. The rain had stopped, but it still felt damp and cold. "Where're we going, dad?"

"I don't know yet, pumpkin. I'll know when I see it. Keep going ok." Tonight, they slept in the open under a tree. It was wet, and it wasn't safe, but they survived. They were running low on food, but they still had two blankets. "Dad?"

"Yes."

"When are we going to find it?"

"I don't know pumpkin. But d'you know what?"

"What?"

"I think I know what we're looking for."

"What is it?"

"The little house on the prairie."

"The little house? What is a prairie, dad?"

"It's an old television series. You won't know it."

"What's a television series?"

"It's something you watch. It's not real. But it looks real. It tells you a story but a story in pictures. Pumpkin, you would probably not understand if I explained it to you. But trust me, it was something very nice that took people away from reality for a while. The little house on the prairie was telling a story about a family who lived on a farm."

"What's a farm?"

"It is a big piece of land, with a house and animals like chickens and pigs. A place where we would be safe. It would be too far away from anybody. So, people wouldn't come to take things away from us."

"That sounds nice. Away from a city?"

"Yes, far, far away." The wind blew autumn leaves over their feet, and the girl laughed. She bent her head watching her feet shuffle through them. Her face looked oddly concentrated as if it was the most critical thing in the world to do. There was a sense of curiosity in her eyes. An expression of childish surprise, and the man realised there was hope. She hadn't lost herself yet. Her clothes were dirty. She wore jeans and a red shirt, but the colour had faded. It was too small for her. He thought he heard something, and his head jerked, but it turned out to be just the shuffling of her feet kicking the leaves. When she discovered how easy it was, she shrieked in excitement. The surrounding trees made them feel secure. It was a false sense of security. They knew, but it felt nice and they tried to cling on to it. The girl stopped kicking the leaves and looked up at her father, full of wonder and love, with her eyes shiny, bright and full of life. It made him almost feel like he could do anything for her. But he couldn't be there forever. He had to find a place for her to stay and people who would take care of her. He remembered back when they were still trying to survive in the city. The chaos, the violence, the crowds and their noise and bad smells. He had tried to find the forest. But it wasn't easy. It had taken them a long time to get there. He could still remember the shock of having to adjust to such a different life, but it happened quick. He hadn't even thought about it, and he was too young at the time to realise what the world would change into. He never had the time to get used to all the new things. He just survived. A lot of the people he knew didn't. He remembered everything always being crowded, the fear, the fights for food, space, even simple things like a thin mattress for a night. The running away from home and the confusion that followed. The horrible feeling of laying down with strangers in camps where the entire floor was covered with mattresses and people. Most of the time he had been lucky. He wasn't tall, and he had never liked fights. He just knew how to get out of the way and use opportunities. But there was one memory trying to creep back which he kept fighting. He pushed it back down into the dark corners of his mind. He concentrated on what he could deal with. The whole city had changed in an instant. They broke shop windows, the streets were littered with huge piles of rubbish, and soon the rats didn't hide anymore. It was a nightmare, one that never seemed to end. The government had vanished or so it had seemed. Whatever they did hadn't affect the people he had met. Hope for help had vanished quickly. And he remembered the times when all he wanted to do was just lay there and die. Letting people do to him what they had done time and time again. But somehow, he had always got going. And finding a friend and fighting together changed everything. Life was still complicated and strange and dangerous. And the fact they had been only just kids hadn't changed, but it made the fighting easier.

The man bent down and began picking up stones. He felt them with his fingertips and started throwing them up in the air. Two birds flew past him, and the girl followed them with their eyes. She waved at them, and the movement of their wings looked like they were waving back. The man began to cry. The girl looked at him. "What is it daddy?"

"Don't worry, pumpkin. Everything will be alright. I just thought… well, the… the sky above… It's still the same." The girl looked up. "The same as what?" The man smiled. He had himself under control now, wiping away his tears with an angry movement of his hand. They were of no use. "The same as it was when I was your age. Everything will be all right, pumpkin", he said, but he wasn't looking into her eyes. It wasn't until now, having a moment to himself, being able to rest and contemplating about the past he realised they hadn't moved forward. Maybe they never would. He ran his left hand across his forehead. The skin felt damp with sweat. He didn't think he would be ill. He couldn't afford it. They couldn't afford it. He wasn't supposed to be sick. Not before he found something for them to stay permanently. Somewhere safe. The girl's shiny eyes watched him again. She could sense something was wrong, but she didn't know what it was. She started kicking the leaves again. Maybe it was some escapism or just plain old childhood fun. Her father looked at her, holding her hand. "The house on the prairie, yes that's what we'll find. A place far, far away where nobody can find to us. You know, pumpkin. Maybe we need to make a plan. A real plan. A plan for the future. I'm sure there aren't that many people around anymore."

"You mean the bad guys are all dead?" She didn't gaze up still kicking the leaves into little piles.

"Maybe not all of them but a lot. They produced nothing. They just took what was already there. And these things… well, most of them would have gone by now. These people grow nothing. They just destroy."

"Dad?"

"Yes."

"We grow nothing either. And we're still alive."

18th of September 2021 London Shepards Bush- Stanlake Road
Benazir

He had to leave to protect Aisha. Now. He turned around having one last glance at his house. A sigh escaped his lips. He would miss his Xbox. They might be away for quite some time. But when they would come back, he would make sure to get the new Horizon game. Aisha started to stir, and he realised he forgot to pack some nappies but they would have to make do without them. He couldn't go back. The banging and shouting had started again, and this time it sounded like they would get in. Benazir started to run. He knew the way out, and all the little alleyways he could get through unseen. At the time he had discovered them it had seemed fun and adventurous, but now it was a matter of life and death. He didn't think when he made his way forward, sliding past the parked cars, hiding behind them and finally reaching a little spot behind a few bushes, which looked like a rubbish tip if you didn't know the area. It was a place where he used to play as a little boy. This seemed to be a lifetime ago. He had prayed for stupid things like a dog or attention from his mother. He never had to pray for his life and that of his sister. That had changed. He shook his head remembering how naïve he had been. They were screwed if there wasn't a miracle. So, he laid his little sister on the ground and started to pray. He wasn't sure if he prayed in the right direction towards

Mekka, but he thought it didn't matter, not today, not now. He began to understand how serious the situation could become. It was bad enough now, but if the police or the forces couldn't get these hateful people under control, it could all end up in a blow. He could feel an undercurrent of growing panic rising inside him, and he tried to suppress it. It wasn't good. For a second he lost his temper and angrily kicked a brick lying around. But he wasn't an angry boy and felt silly straight away. His sister started to cry. He had startled her. All that mattered was where they could go to spend the next few days. He picked up Aisha, rocking her back and forth. She seemed to like it. He realised he didn't know a lot about babies. She seemed to be ok for the moment. She wasn't hungry yet and his mother had changed Aisha's nappies before they had killed her. But he knew enough to realise that babies needed a lot of looking after and they enjoyed making themselves known, even if it was a very well-behaved childlike his sister. He needed to go somewhere where it didn't matter when she cried. Somewhere where people didn't know he was a Muslim or at least they didn't care. Maybe this was some test. Maybe the end of the world was coming and he, Benazir, was being tested if he was worthy to survive. "Nonsense", he almost shouted. Allah wouldn't test him like that. Not with Aisha. She was a baby. She had done nothing that deserved punishment or some test. He began strolling across the place, always keeping within the shadows of the bushes. What happened next occurred in a matter of seconds. He was trying to walk over a pile patch of rubbish made of tins and old take away cartons when a guy, wearing a red baseball cap and a green t-shirt, jumped in front of him. Well, he didn't jump. It looked as if someone had pushed him. He was cradling his chest, moaned and his eyes caught Benazir's. His lips formed the words "help", but no sound escaped. He stretched out his hand and just collapsed on the ground. Nothing. No movement. No sound. Nothing. Was he dead? For a second Benazir hoped he was, so he didn't have to do anything. He wouldn't know what, but then he called himself an idiot, realising as an Imam he would probably have to attend injured or dying people lots of times. And he needed to be able to be there for them, to give them hope. He stepped closer. The man on the floor still didn't move. Benazir touched him with his foot like he would a dog who he worried might bite him. The guy still didn't react. Benazir bent down, still cradling his sister and tried to turn the man, but the guy was too heavy. He put his sister on the floor again. *If he kept doing that, she might catch a cold.* He used both hands and all his strength to turn him. He didn't speak, and he didn't dare to say something. Somehow it didn't seem to be the right place, and he couldn't find the right words. The man was dead. His open eyes stared at the sky. There was a lot of blood on his hands and his chest. It covered his trousers. Benazir struggled to accept what he was seeing. It must be a nightmare from which he would wake up at any minute. His jaw hung open and his face was grey. What was he meant to do? He started to panic. "Shit. Shit. Shit." He stared at the body in disbelief. *Aisha.* The thought brought him back to his senses. She needed him. She was alive. He could do nothing for this man and needed to get away from this place. The killer would be very close. *Run. Now. As long as you still have the chance.* His mind tried to force him to get away. But Benazir had to think about his options. At the moment he still hid in the shadows and Aisha was quiet. The only one who was aware he was here was the guy in front of him and he was dead. Who was he? Was he being followed? Had he been attacked randomly and ran away or had someone tried to kill him specifically? If it was the second, his attacker would be near him trying to make sure the guy was dead. If it was a random attack Benazir could probably just get up and try to find a safe place for him and Aisha. He had to decide. If he sat here, he might freeze to death. The boy risked it and just stepped over the dead guy. He staggered over uneven, muddy ground and just stopped once or twice to make sure Aisha was ok, looking around and checking if someone was following them. *Nothing.* He walked silently, trying to get to grips with what he had recently witnessed. Could Allah really want this? He still wasn't sure where they would go. He felt like there was something, somewhere they could go but the idea hadn't quite come to him yet. It was still lingering in his unconscious mind. He was trying to force it out, but it resisted. They kept away from the main roads, frequently he spotted a fire in the distance and heard gunshots. Sometimes there was shouting but most of the time Benazir just heard screams. He realised carrying a rucksack had been a bright idea. Alisha started to feel too heavy for his arms and he wouldn't have been able to carry a bag in his hands. They just kept going. He wished he would have packed more practical things, drinks and food and nappies for Aisha. Maybe they would have to spend the night outside. But he thought he would find these things somewhere as long as he was alive. He couldn't have done any more than what he had done. He hadn't even packed his mobile phone but who could he have called, anyway. None of his friends could provide a safe place tonight. They were all in as much danger as Benazir and Aisha were. They were all like him. He yearned for the warm morning sun but he would still have to wait a few hours until sunrise. He looked ahead just contemplating. How could he ever go back? His friends could all be dead, even if they restored order somehow. His family didn't live in England. He had never been a fan of big family gatherings in the past and it had suited him fine but now he wished there would be someone they could go to. Even if they were also in danger tonight. But at least Benazir would have some goal, some place the two of them could head towards. Suddenly it was almost as if someone had switched the light on in his mind. All his friends were like him living in the same area. All but one. Mark. Ok, he wasn't his best friend, but they always got along. His parents had seemed to like him the few times Benazir had been at their house. His mum hadn't said too much but Mark's dad had been friendly.

It's at least half a mile, he imagined. But it was doable from here. Only half a mile and him and Aisha could be safe. A beautiful upper-class suburban area where nobody would search for him, trying to hunt him down. The shadows were lengthening across the street, and everything seemed to be strangely quiet. But he had to get back onto the roads to reach his goal.

He smiled. Yes, they would make it. He stepped over a piece of wire almost catching his foot in it. The ground was overgrown with nettles in between the rubbish. There were just so many things one could stumble over and get caught in. Benazir started to walk slower. It would be no good if he would fall and knock himself out. Aisha would just die. She had nobody else.

Half a mile began to seem like a lot, but the boy told himself it wasn't. He sat down on a big stone trying to adjust the way his sister was laying in his arms. He needed to catch his breath. It felt like they had been walking for hours but all sense for time had slipped away. He just sat, looking at Aisha sleeping, cradling her. They could just sit here forever. It felt right. No, they wouldn't. Benazir forced himself to get up. His legs ached, but he tried to ignore it. Maybe someone was already looking for him and Aisha. But that was dreaming. His dad had always made sure they wouldn't get too close to anybody. Benazir now understood why. His father hadn't wanted anybody to find out what he was doing. With all these meetings he had always made sure that no-one else would be in the house. Someone who might sneak around. Someone who wasn't as trusting as Benazir. He started shaking his head. How could he not have known? How could he not even have suspected anything? His dad, a terrorist. The boy's eyes looked at Aisha again. They needed to get going. It would be just a little way through. He would just walk and walk and walk until they reached Mark's house. What else could they do?

19th of September 2021 4 am London Shepards Bush
Mark

"Who is this?", T.J. whispered. A pause of two seconds and another quick knock followed. "I don't know", Mark and his mother answered simultaneously. But there was no movement. T.J. didn't share their indecision. He reached quickly for his gun and pointed it at the door. "Who's this?" he shouted. No answer. The next moment a bullet hit the wall beside the door and big pieces of plaster scattered on the floor. Mark's mother shrieked, and a baby started crying. "Stop it", she cried. "Stop shooting. It's a baby. You cannot shoot a baby. It's wrong. Mark and T.J. turned their eyes towards one another trying to understand what the other one was considering. Mark nodded. "She's right. You cannot shoot a baby. It's probably a neighbour trying to hide. T.J. fired again. This time he hit the ceiling. More plaster was coming down. He hadn't aimed at something in particular, and the bullet had hit the ceiling light. It was dark in an instant. Only the lights from the kitchen were shining from the left. A surprised grunting sound escaped his lips. Mark stumbled back dragging his mother with him. "I don't want to shoot you. It just went off. I'm sorry." T.J. frowned which created a confused expression on his face. Obviously, he wasn't too familiar with using a gun even though he pretended to be in control and had killed a policeman. At the time it had seemed effortless. "I think we should just let her in." It was strange, but somehow hierarchies had changed. T.J. didn't seem to be the leader anymore. Mark stepped forward. "Ok." Perhaps that was the problem. This guy had just played too many computer games and shooting a woman, and her baby was never part of it. "I will open the door now, ok. Put the gun down." T.J. didn't do that, but he pointed it to the floor. It was enough. Since his brother had died, and he had seen two other people die Mark's understanding of how things should be seemed to have changed. Maybe he was seeing himself as someone who had to act instead of just watch and let so-called adults do everything. Things had changed, even if order was reinstalled tomorrow or in a few days, he had changed and become detached from ordinary rules. He stepped forward and took the gun from T.J.'s hands curling up his lips in disgust. Even if he was to die now did it matter? The thought didn't worry him. He didn't suspect anybody would help him. He had to do it by himself and maybe teaming up with a mother and her baby would matter. If only he could convince his mum to keep away from T.J. He opened the door and stared. "It's one of them", T.J. growled and Mark's mother started screaming. "Shut up," Mark told them quietly. "He's not. It's only a normal boy with dark hair. I know him. He goes to my school. He's been here before. You know him as well and you liked him. Stop acting like an idiot." He aimed it at his mother, and it did the trick. She wasn't used to him speaking like that. She didn't tell him off, but she stopped screaming. Of one thing Mark was certain. This boy needed his help, and Mark would make sure nothing happened to him. Not with his baby sister in his arms.

Mark had never fired a gun before. But he would if he had too just like they did in the videogames. "Come in,", he just mumbled." His body turned around. "This is Ben, a friend of mine." He paused looking at the gun in his hand. "Ben, would you mind shutting the door behind you?" Mark felt uncomfortable being stuck in the middle between his friend, his mother, who had lost her marbles and T.J. But he had to pretend everything was just fine, if he didn't want the situation to escalate. His mother said something unintelligible. Her hands audibly scratched the wall behind him. "What was that?", Mark asked menacingly. "Your mouth really must be dry from all the screaming." He walked towards his mother. "Mum, she's a baby." She smiled and nodded. He pointed to a chair. "Ben why don't you go to the kitchen and see if you can find something to eat and drink. You must be starving."

Mark's mother opened her mouth. "There are nappies and baby formula in the big cupboard. I keep them for when my sister comes with her little one." She stepped forward, and her voice sounded less shaky. "I will not kill a boy and his baby sister." She walked forward with her arms outstretched, trying to hug Mark. For one moment they all stood still. They could hear the chaos outside, the people, cars and languages hard to understand. Mark's first instinct was to step back but love took over. He rubbed his eyes, only wanting comfort. For a moment they were just mother and son embracing each other. Mark was the first to let go. It was just a matter of time when things would kick off. His mother might not want to fight anymore, but there was no guarantee this might not change and T.J.… well, he didn't know the guy. He seemed beaten and tired, but maybe he just pretended to be because he didn't have his gun anymore. And that wasn't the only problem he expected. They couldn't stay here forever. A day or two wouldn't be a problem. But what if it took the armed forces longer to put everything back in place? He had no more trust that the police could manage on their own. The government would call for help if chaos continued. Everybody seemed so unhinged. He looked around. It looked like finally, people had attacked and he was standing there, amongst it. His family was just an example of what was going on everywhere.

The television was still running. Mark could hear every word. It was like a war zone out there. "Ok." He sighed. It looks like we're all going to stay here tonight or should I say today. Nobody has to stay. You're all free to leave. But if we are staying together, we will play nicely. Nobody will hurt anybody. Is that understood?" No-one said anything. "I said is that understood?" Everyone in the room mumbled something that sounded like a yes or agreement. There wasn't anything else constructive to do. So, for now, the boy stepped back, checking that there was no clear sign of someone trying to do something stupid and went to the kitchen.

Benazir was just sitting there with Aisha in his arms. He hadn't looked for any food or the nappies for Aisha. The little girl was awake and was making sounds showing she didn't feel comfortable but she didn't cry anymore. Maybe she had no strength left in her little body. Benazir was a mess. His face was dirty, and his clothes had marks from some strange liquid all over it. Maybe it was vomit, but it didn't reek. Mark noticed nothing from where he was standing. "Benazir? Are you alright?" He offered his hand, trying to touch his friend. Benazir didn't answer, still cradling his sister who was making some strange but quiet noises now. "Is that Aisha? Where's your mum, Benazir?" Nothing. "Can I hold her? I think maybe she needs changing and I'm sure she's hungry."

"Yes." No more. That's all he said. But what did it mean? Yes, you can hold her. Yes, she's hungry or needs changing. Mark just stepped forward to take Aisha and noticed he was still holding the gun. Maybe that scared Benazir. He put it on the kitchen table and held out his hands to take Aisha. Benazir looked at him with his big black eyes, his body shaking.

"I will not harm her I promise. Please. She needs looking after."

"Why can't your mum do it?" More words. Thank god.

"She's still in shock. My brother has died today and… my dad." Mark just stated the fact. "She cannot cope with anything right now."

"Your brother? But you aren't a Muslim. They're just shooting Muslims tonight."

"Who told you that?"

"No-one. I just thought. Mh… I watched TV today, and it was… it was… Muslims that did all this. Big Ben and all these people."

"I know. But it's not the first time. It's been going on for years. I think it's everyone now. People hated each other for so long and today they have the chance to kill. A lot of them do."

"How did it happen?"

"What?"

"Your dad?"

Mark swallowed a big lump in his throat. "Someone shot him through a window, and it hit his head. Where's your dad? I don't think I have ever met him."

"No, you haven't."

"Well, where's he and… your… mum?"

"My mum's dead."

"And your dad? You can find him, right? He'll look after you."

"He's… dead I mean. They killed him." It was difficult for Benazir to lie. Imams didn't lie. But he had to. He just couldn't tell the truth. And really, it wasn't a lie, anyway. They had killed his father. With shaky hands, he fumbled some notes out of his pocket. "Here have this. It's just twenty Pounds, but it will pay for the nappies and the milk. "I'm sorry to bother you. I am. But I didn't know where else to go tonight. I'm not ready for this and don't think I'll ever be ready for something like this. This boy. The big one. He hates me. He hates people like me. Maybe it was a bad idea to—"

"Benazir, stop," Mark interrupted. "You can do this. We can do it. Let's just stick together. And help will be here soon. I have a gun, and I'll not let anybody hurt you or Aisha. Do you understand? It will be tough, but we can handle it together. It'll just be tonight, and tomorrow everything will be back to normal. You're very strong."

Tears sprang to Marks' eyes, but he just wiped them off with an angry gesture. "Try to relax. Okay. I'll take care of Aisha and I can ask my mum to help. She likes babies. Put on the kettle mate and make some tea. There's hot chocolate in the cupboard as well if you prefer."

"How did your brother, how did Brian die?"

Mark just looked at him. "It was an accident. He walked into a flying bullet."

"What? They killed your brother but why? He's so small. That's crazy."

"No," Mark shook his head. "They didn't mean to shoot him."

Who was that bullet aimed at?"

Pause. Mark sighed. "I don't know. People were just going crazy."

"I'm sorry. I'm too nosy. But Brian. He's your brother. I know how I feel about Aisha. I know she's just a baby, but it's nice to have a sibling. Someone who you belong to."

Mark just shrugged. If he would say any more, he would burst into tears. Benazir looked at him with his curious eyes. "My prediction is though–this will not be over by tomorrow. And you know I'm right." There was a smile in his voice. It was crooked and out of place. But Mark chuckled, wiping his eyes. "Right. Whatever. I will change Aisha. But everything will be alright."

"I hope so."

"I know so." Mark was concentrating now. He was good at changing nappies, having done it quite a few times with his cousin, but this was different. He needed to make sure his mother and T.J. were not planning anything. In her state of mind, he couldn't ask her for help.

He finished changing Aisha, walked towards the kitchen door and stopped. "Mum?" Nothing. "Mum?"

"Yes?" A big sigh of relief washed over Mark. He walked back into the living room, forgetting about the gun which was still on the kitchen table. "Mum, I just changed the baby, but I need something to put her in. You know a basket or something. Do you have any idea what I could use?"

"Yes… you know… there's still a big picnic basket under the stairs. I'll get it. It should be big enough." His mother's voice drifted up from where she was sitting. She smiled at Mark. But the smile disappeared in an instant. Her eyes widened, looking at something behind her son. "No. Don't."

Mark turned around in one agile move, but T.J. was quicker. The teenager wanted the gun, and he was quick. But not fast enough. Benazir jumped up and got to it first pulling the trigger.

Ross-on-Wye, Herefordshire

Five years later

"Pumpkin. That's different; we aren't bad people."

"I know, but daddy, if we're still alive, they might be."

"I know, but these people don't come to the woods. There's nothing here for them. They don't know what you can and what you can't eat. You can't grow anything here deliberately. It just grows, or it doesn't. If some of these people are still alive, they will still be in the cities."

Autumn fog hung in the air covering the man's words. There wasn't a breath of wind, and apart from a few birds, there was complete silence. The man looked around. They would need to find a permanent home. Winter would start soon. He could already see a thin layer of frost covering the ground in the mornings. It melted away quick as soon as the sun came out but it was there. Every surface, every leaf, every centimetre of ground was covered now since the week had begun. It looked beautiful when the man got up long before his daughter woke. But beauty was deceiving. It would soon be deadly. The girl looked at him. "Dad. Are you ok?"

He forced a smile. "I'm ok. Why did you stop playing with the leaves? It's fun isn't it?" "Yes, it was, but we can't stay here," the girl replied. It occurred to him how much wiser she was than her age would show. They couldn't stay here, but they could also not risk moving in the dark. If the fog stayed, it would make it impossible to see danger early enough. They needed to find something now. But at least they were lucky in some respect. The fog began to lift already. It didn't want to linger and make their lives even more of a misery. Also, the moon had illuminated things. The man hoped it would show them a way to a place they could stay and if possible, not just for one night. But something seemed wrong. Maybe it was just his suspicious mind, which was always on alert, always checking out potential danger. He wasn't a soldier. All he wanted was to find out how to heal people. Make them feel better. And he was good at it. Before he could think about it anymore, the girl pulled his hand. "What is it?" he asked. She looked at him, dead calm. She wasn't moving. "Let's follow the moon," she said. The fog had now thinned. "Follow the moon?" he whispered.

"Yes. Or do you know where else we can go?" He sat down, not looking too convinced. "Any other suggestions?" He looked at her.

"No, sorry. At least it won't be dark."

"I guess that's good, and a great advice pumpkin. And if we meet someone… well not everyone wants to hurt us. Most people struggle themselves trying to find a safe place. Some will return to where they come from. Many people are just camping outside. You remember these nice people we met two weeks ago, right? The ones who let us sleep in their tent."

"Yes, they stole my granola bar, but they were nice. They didn't hurt us. The woman looked very sad. I think something bad had happened to her. And the man mumbled in his sleep."

"Oh, I don't know. Maybe she was just tired of fighting all the time."

They'd had this conversation before, and it led nowhere. The girl sighed. "We better hurry. Let's go. We need to find somewhere to stay." The man glanced down at her. "I guess you're right. He picked up her little rucksack and put it on her back. He took her hand, grinning at her, crooked and radiantly, but said nothing.

"Look", the girl suddenly shouted and pointed her finger at something. His gaze followed her hand, and his heart jumped with joy. A bush full of blackberries. Why hadn't they seen it before? Well, it didn't matter. There were enough for them not to go hungry tonight. The girl shrieked. She didn't jog. Instead, she walked as fast as she could to get to the berries. She picked them quickly and expertly. When she finally spoke again, her mouth all smeared and red with berry juice. She used words he'd never heard her say out loud. It felt as if someone lodged something in her mind, something hard and unyielding, and something she couldn't express. It made him want to scream. "Dad is this ever going to end. I mean us looking for food, being scared, going hungry or being sick?"

"Yes, it is. And it will end soon. We will follow the moon and the river, and we will find something, away from everybody. Something where we will be safe. And tonight, we will walk towards it. We might not find it tonight, but maybe tomorrow. He smiled again, but it disappeared quickly when a flash of light caught his eye, only a few metres in front of them, and a reflection of something. It was only there for a fraction of a second, but his alarm bells rang. He pulled his daughter down, and they cowered on the ground not saying anything for a few seconds. "Did you see that?" he whispered.

"No, what was it?"

"I'm not sure. Something shiny. I think someone's there." He put one arm around her, pulling the girl tighter towards him. There was a whining sound, followed by silence. They held their breaths and listened harder. Nothing. Wait, a vague, scraping noise. The moon had come out now, and the forest wasn't pitch black, but it wasn't lit up either. They could see enough to move, but they couldn't make out any great detail in the distance. Shuffling. A yelping sound. The man pulled out his gun. The blackberry bushes in front of them moved. "What is it?" the girl whispered with a thin, high voice.

"Quiet." The bush moved again; its leaves and thorns being pushed aside by a big black nose and a furry snout. Dark eyes were looking at them curiously. "Oh, daddy. It's a dog. Looks like the shiny thing were his eyes. It's only a dog. Can we keep him?" A wave of relief washed over the man; his mind started working again. It wasn't a huge dog, but it wasn't small either. What if it was aggressive or carried any diseases? But it didn't look like it wanted to bite anybody. It was just peering at the two of them.

"He's alone", the girl grinned. "Please, can we keep him?"

19th of September 2021 London Shepards Bush- Stanlake Road
Benazir and Mark

Silence. For a moment everyone stood still. T.J. collapsed. There was a thudding sound when his body hit the floor, but apart from that–nothing. Mark and Benazir just stared. Mark's mother started screaming.

"Mum, shut up. I need to think. "Mark remained calm. The boy did not understand how he did it. Maybe his mind was in shock. Perhaps he had seen too much already tonight, and there were no emotions left. He didn't worry about it. When his mother didn't stop, he slapped her face, and that stopped her.

"Mark." It was a quiet sound that came from Benazir. He didn't say more. But Mark understood. Don't become like them. These people who had no love. Mark suddenly remembered his childhood which had stopped this morning. His childhood that was so full of dirt, toys, pets, his brother, his friends and above all love. He had always felt loved by his mum and dad. There had been no sign of hate there, and maybe… maybe he just hadn't seen it. Maybe he had just ignored the little snide remarks here and there, the jokes when they came across someone who wasn't white and had a different religion. Something that seemed normal at the time because it wasn't too bad and the jokes had seemed funny. They accepted his friends, all of them but had they seen them as equal, especially his mother? He looked at her. Her staring gaze made him shiver. "Mum, I'm sorry. I'm so sorry. But they're killing people out there."

"They're killing people in here. Well, at least he does… this… this one." She almost spat out the words. "He did it in self-defence, mum. You saw it. T.J. would kill him."

"Does it matter? He will kill us anyway."

"Mum, Benazir is my friend, you know him and he has to look after his baby sister. He won't kill anybody."

"He just did and how do you know what he will do in a few years' time when he's a man. He might even kill his sister if she doesn't obey him. Maybe she doesn't want to marry the man her family chooses and… bang."

"Mam, I would never kill my sister. She's all I've got left. I just want peace." Benazir's had quietly walked in the bright-lit living room, his face was wet with tears, but his voice remained calm.

"Mark, I'm begging you. You cannot be friends with one of them. No matter how nice he's now. Don't you understand what's been going on? The world's at war. And if we team up with one of them, we'll lose." Mark's jaw tightened. "Mum, we've lost already. Dad's been killed, Brian's dead, and Ben's parents have died. We're in this together. This isn't about belonging to a group. It's about sticking together to survive tonight and maybe a few more days until the police will fix everything."

As soon as the words were out of his mouth, he realised they were a lie. They would fix nothing. Not that way. But he was still only a thirteen-year-old boy and even though he had to grow up fast, he was still hoping like only a child could that had grown up in peace.

"So, what are we going to do?" Benazir looked at him as if his friend was an adult and not a boy the same age as him. "Well, I guess we need to get some sleep. Mum…", Mark looked at her, reasoning and almost saying sorry with his eyes. She knew what it meant. He didn't trust her. She loved him and he loved her but her son didn't trust her anymore. However, she understood. She feared herself and would sleep here tonight, in her own house, probably with the help of a few pills but she wouldn't be able to get out of her room. Her hand wiped her blond curls of her face. Her son would lock her in like an insane person who couldn't make rational judgements. And maybe he was right. "I can't leave Brian." It was one last and desperate attempt, but Mark didn't have any of it. "He will stay here. I put a blanket on him, and I'll give him his favourite toy." She stepped closer to him. "He's my little boy." He stepped back as if she had a contagious disease. She moved forward again sighing. "I just want to say goodnight." Her fingers brushed his face. She wanted to kiss him. "Maybe everything will be alright. Maybe." Her voice was dead, hopeless. She watched his face relax, loosen. But it didn't make her feel better. How could this have happened? How could she lose two sons and a husband in one night? Even though his face was smoother now, suspicion and misgiving lingered in his eyes. He stood up straight, and for a short moment, he appeared thoughtful, as if he would change his mind. But that moment went quickly. He looked into her eyes. "Goodnight. Mum. Let's go upstairs." His mother began to say something, but he raised a hand, and, avoiding her gaze, he whispered frankly, "I have to do this mum. You know it. And when all this is over, we will get help. Together." Benazir looked nervously at them but said nothing. His eyes just followed them when they walked up the stairs. He was holding the gun. He listened to the footsteps in the room above, one heavy and slurred, the other lighter, stopping, moving and stopping again. He could hear muted words passing, but he didn't understand what was being said. A squeak, a door being shut and the rattle of a key as it looked the upstairs master bedroom. The light set of footsteps returned, hesitated for a moment and came down. Benazir saw his friend pocketing the key, and his fingers tightened on the gun. "Leave it, Ben. Please. No more killing tonight, ok." And Benazir obeyed. "Ok, Mark, I think you need some sleep as well. We don't know what will happen in the next few days, well we don't even know what'll happen in the next few hours. We don't know when we're going to get some uninterrupted sleep again. "Mark, I'm scared. I'm scared to be in this house with all these…" The boy just looked at Benazir. "Me too. But we have to wait. I covered them all up and tomorrow someone will come and tell us what to do. Can you stay awake for a few more hours?"

"Yes. I think so."

"Ok, I'm going upstairs to my room. Can you wake me in about four hours?"

"Sure." Mark turned around to go back upstairs.

"Ehm, Mark."

"Yes?"

"Where's your room? I mean I've never been upstairs."

2Oh, sorry. It's the first one on the right. Go up the stairs, and it's the door with the big 'no entry' sticker."

"Ok, thanks. Mark?"

"Yes."

"Are we friends?"

Mark turned around looking at him and swallowed. "I'm not sure. I don't know. But I don't want to kill you. That has to be enough for tonight."

"Sure, it's enough… for tonight." Mark nodded and went upstairs. Benazir could hear him locking his door soon after.

Ross-on-Wye, Herefordshire

Five years later

"Please? I mean look at him. He's so cute. He's just curious. He's not even scared. I'm sure he's just looking for a friend."

"How d'you know it's a he?"

The girl smiled. "I don't. But he looks like a boy. Don't you think? We can always have a look. Come here, boy." She squatted down. "Here boy, here." She stretched out her hand.

"No, don't. He might carry something."

"Carry what? He carries nothing, look? It's just fur."

The man laughed out loud. "No, pumpkin. I mean he might carry disease. This fluff ball might be ill, and he could make us ill."

"Daddy, he doesn't look ill." The dog had come closer now and started licking the girl's hand. She giggled. "Ha, ha, please stop it. Ha, ha. That tickles. Sammy. No."

And that's what did it for the man. He had never heard such a carefree laugh coming from her. He didn't want her to stop. Her laughter was like music to his ears. He tried to listen to it repeatedly. "Ok. Maybe. You're right. He doesn't look ill. But he must eat and pumpkin you know we haven't got enough food. Not even for the two of us." The girl stood up and went to her father. She stroked his arm. "We'll manage. We'll find something. There's always something. And Sammy survived, didn't he? So, he probably found enough food for himself, anyway. Look. He probably hunts. And if he does that, he might find food for us." The man reached down and took her hand. The girl smiled. "So, we keep him?" Her dad sighed. She almost had him. "And also, he's big. Big. He'll probably protect us from bad people."

"Maybe, he will. But pumpkin. Don't worry too much about the bad people. I think there aren't too many left…"

"I know", she interrupted him impatiently pulling his hand. "You said they're probably dead by now. Fighting over the last few cans of food and all that."

"Yes, but it's not only that. You know what happened a few years back? I'm not sure you'll remember. You're still small, and you were even smaller back then. A lot of things exploded."

"I know." She shouted impatiently. The dog cowered. "Don't worry Sammy. It's ok." She stroked his thick fur. I remember, daddy. The big bang. That's what you're talking about, right? People were so scared. Everyone was talking about it. I didn't understand what was going on, but I know I was petrified because everybody else was. You were. What was it daddy? I think I will understand it now. I know there's nothing to worry about now, but what was it?"

"Well, bang is the right word. And you're right you don't need to worry about it now. But you know, the lights. I mean you remember the lights, right? I mean in the shops and the houses. Or maybe this was before you were old enough to remember."

"Lights? You mean fires?"

"No, no fires. I mean electric lights."

"Electric? No, I don't know." She bit her lips.

"Yeah, I guess you were still a baby or maybe a toddler. You see before everything changed just after you were born. People lived in houses which had… well, buttons on the wall. You've seen them, the houses I mean. Probably didn't pay much attention to the switches. We always had to be quick and always went in during the day. You remember that. And when they came home…"

"Home from where?"

"Well, home from work or seeing friends or school…"

"School?"

"Yes, kids used to go there to learn. I'll explain it to you later. Anyway, they came home, and when it was late and dark, they could push these buttons, and the house lit up."

"Lit up? You mean, they burned down?"

"Ha, ha. No, pumpkin. They didn't burn down. I mean… Ah, I know. You remember the lights on that bicycle a few weeks ago. The man was cycling down the road, past us and his front light was shining in your eyes."

"Yes, yes", she said excitedly. "It was bright."

"Exactly, and these lights… Well, people used to have them in their houses."

"Wow, all their houses? That's a lot of lights and a lot of batteries. But people ran out of batteries."

"I know, but when I was younger, and you hadn't been born yet, people could still charge these batteries, again and again, and again. But batteries didn't feed these lights in the houses."

"No batteries? What made them light up?"

"Ah, well pumpkin." The man took a deep breath in and his hand touched the girl's head, patting it absentmindedly. "It's complicated. But they were attached to something called wires, and they were very long wires. They ended in places called factories and these factories produced power."

"What's power? Is it light?"

"Well, sort of. Anyway, People could produce this power in various ways. They could either burn coal, gas or they used so-called nuclear power plants. I had to do a paper once in school about these when I was a boy. But you've never been to school." He sighed. "Well, anyway, these nuclear power plants worked very well, but when they broke down, they were very dangerous."

"They exploded?"

"Yes."

"How did they produce power, daddy? Could we start them again? I mean in cars, you don't just have lights, you can also play music and turn on the heating. To have that in a house would be nice. But cars need a battery, and they always run out at some point. I remember our car. It was nice."

"Yes, it was."

"Maybe in the cities, they've already got power again, and the lights are coming on, and it's warm in the winter."

"I don't think so, pumpkin. It's a lot of work to get everything up and running, and I don't think there are enough skilled people left. You see most of these nuclear reactors or power plants boiled water to produce power or electricity. They worked with something called harnessing nuclear fission. I don't know the details of it. I just remember that word from reading it somewhere and from what other people told me."

"The scared people?"

"Yes, the scared people. Well's very complicated, and I don't understand it myself, but a lot of things happen that produce a steady supply of heat to boil water, drive turbines and generate electricity for lights and other things. But as nice as it is, it's hazardous when it goes wrong and if there aren't enough people to look after it and make sure it doesn't get overheated it just…"

"Explodes. And people die."

"Yes. But sometimes it's not so much what happens when the power plant explodes because that wouldn't be so bad if you're not near the explosion. The problem is radioactivity. You cannot see it, but it makes you very ill. And without something to cool it, such a reactor will continuously boil off the water until there is no more water. This water surrounds some radioactive rods which are made from a special material, and they may melt. And if nobody stops it, hot radioactive fuel can melt through the steel vessel and other barriers."

"And this radio… radioca…"

"Radioactivity."

"Yes, this radioactivity runs out and makes people ill."

"That's right."

"But you still have to be close to that power plant, right?"

"Yes, but not as close as you have to be to be affected by an explosion. This radioactivity travels. The wind pushes it further. And because people couldn't see it…"

"They didn't run away and became very ill."

"That's right."

"Does it kill dogs as well?"

"What?"

"Well, you said it makes people ill, and they might even die, but what about dogs? What about Sammy?"

"Don't worry about Sammy. He'll be ok. This happened a few years ago. I don't think we're anywhere near an old nuclear reactor."

"Daddy, do you know someone who died of this? Is that why you read these medical books all the time?"

"Maybe. You see when I was a little boy, I wanted to become a doctor, and a good friend of mine died, and I couldn't help him so I started reading as much as I could so this would never happen again. But these books will not help with radioactivity, and even if I was a real doctor, there is nothing I could do about it."

"But all these factories are quiet now. I mean if they exploded this happened already. So, we don't need to worry about the wind blowing something towards Sammy, right?"

"Right." He didn't tell her there was something much worse than nuclear reactors.

"Daddy, you know what. I think we could sleep outside tonight if we can't find anything else and cover ourselves with branches like we've done before and Sammy will look after us. I'm just too tired to walk around looking for a prairie."

"Maybe you're right, pumpkin." He sighed, and for just a moment he didn't care what would happen to them. His legs ached, and he realised they wouldn't find what they were looking for. No matter how bright the moon was tonight. They did what the girl had suggested and Sammy just laid there not making any noise, as if he knew their life depended on it. The girl smiled in her dreams, and the man had nightmares about lumps of hair falling out, boils, sores and people screaming in pain. But what was the most frightening thing was the sense of helplessness. Knowing he couldn't do anything to help these faceless people.

19th of September 2021 London Shepards Bush- Stanlake Road
Benazir and Mark

"Wake up Mark. It's time."

Nothing.

"Mark." Benazir could hear shuffling noises behind the door, and for a moment he felt like dropping everything and just running away. He was running on empty, and sure he had nodded off in the kitchen even though he was meant to keep watch. Mark's voice sounded muffled and strange coming through the door, "What's wrong?"

"Nothing. You just ask me to wake you up in four hours. It's five now. Sorry."

"Oh, yes." Benazir could hear the door being unlocked. Mark looked at him with tired eyes. His hair stood in all sorts of directions. "It took me a while to fall asleep. Sorry. The bed is all yours." Benazir almost handed over Aisha to him, but he hesitated. "Can you look after her? I mean if you can't I'll take her."

"No, I'm fine. Honest. If she cries, she'll wake you up. You need sleep."

Mark swallowed hard. "Have you heard mum?"

"No, I think the pills knocked her out." Benazir felt like he had said something stupid. "I'm sorry. That sounded real, like… I don't know."

"Hey, don't worry. You're right. Well, she has been taking pills. And saying it nicer doesn't change the fact. She always has taken something of some sort to help her sleep. Not sure if she's an addict. I never thought it was a problem. And it doesn't matter now. It meant we had something in the house to calm her down." He bit his lip as if he wanted to say more. Maybe to defend his mum but he kept silent, just chewing his lips. After a few seconds Mark opened the door wider, walked to the window, pushed the curtains aside a little and looked out across the street. What could be their next step? He hoped everything would turn out alright and maybe it would just because it was a new day. Thoughts like that were a mistake. It was quieter, but people were still running around shouting. Maybe they should start calling them gangs because that's what they appeared to be. Mark looked back at Benazir and shook his head as he raised a hand to put a finger over his mouth. With this gesture, he told his friend it wasn't over and they had to take responsibility for their lives now. Nobody else would do it. "I think you should sleep now, Ben. I'll wake you if something's going on." The boy glanced towards the window again and sighed. For a moment Benazir thought he was about to step forward and open it shouting at everybody outside that two Muslims were hiding in this house, but Mark didn't. He just raised his hand and pointed at his bed saying nothing. Benazir handed over Aisha and removed his shoes and socks, sitting down on the bed. Mark just nodded, walked out of the room and shut the door. Benazir sat there with his hands in his lap and started realising he hadn't given Mark the gun. "Damn", the boy whispered, putting a hand in front of his mouth, realising he shouldn't swear. The sun was shining through the window, and the boy wasn't sure if he could sleep with all the light streaming in, but it didn't take long, and he was fast asleep.

When he opened his eyes again Mark stood inside the room looking at him quietly, his hands folded in front of his stomach. He had small, bony shoulders. There was nothing remarkable about him. Only a boy who wouldn't stand out anywhere. "Do you know that I always wanted to become a doctor", he said. Benazir looked at his friend's unremarkable features, his curly brown hair and the sad blue eyes. The boy's hands tightened on the gun underneath his covers. He had a quick look behind him to the window, but all he could see was Mark's reflection. Benazir's mind was going into overdrive. His friend's words had taken him by surprise. He didn't answer, listening for something else to come. But there was nothing. "No, I didn't know you want to become a doctor. That's… great." It sounded pretty lame but what else could he say? Silence again. All Benazir could hear was the sounds of morning birds. He paused, frightened, no, terrified to say the wrong thing. He sat up. "You can still become a doctor, even a surgeon if you want to. Maybe things will not go back to how it was, but it will become organised again. We'll be able to go back to school, and things will be some kind of normal." But normal was gone. Burned to the ground, shot, bombed.

"Mum's dead."

"What?" It became yet another example of Mark's extraordinariness. Any other kid would have screamed in panic but not him. Maybe he was in shock. "She took too many pills last night. I'm not sure if it was deliberate. I went in there to fix the window and saw her lying there. Tried to make her sick, but it was too late. If I was older… if, I was a doctor I could have saved her." Benazir hated the tone of his voice. It was so lifeless, so unpredictable but if he wanted to be an Iman, he would have to stay calm and be able to listen to people, no matter what they said and how they sounded. He clung to the thought. It saved his sanity.

Nature was calling, and it felt like his bladder would burst any minute, but he didn't dare to tell Mark. Not yet. "How did you fix the window?"

"What?" Mark's eyes seemed bigger.

"The window. You said you went in there to fix the window."

"Oh. That. Yes, I used some wood panels, just nailed them in. Dad…", he swallowed. "Dad had kept them in the garage."

"That's good."

"Yes."

A loud bang interrupted them both. Someone attacked the door with kicks and blows. The whole room shook. They needed to go. Well, he needed to go but he just couldn't. He got up, and they both walked downstairs, one step at a time. "Where's Aisha?", Benazir whispered staring at the lock hoping it would hold. He had visions of the door being flung open and some religious fundamentalist standing there with a triumphant, smiling face, pointing their guns at him. He understood the game these people played. It didn't matter if it was Muslims against Christians, vice versa or any other religions. Belief wasn't important. It was about feeling superior, about violence and frustration. If they would get him, they would just kill him, and if Mark got caught by these people, he would be dead. And now they would punish him if they found out Mark had been hiding a Muslim in his house. There was no doubt about it. "It's them or us, Mark."

The game had begun. "Do you still have the gun, Ben and is it still loaded?" The sound of fear in Mark's voice implied panic. And deep down This time Benazir he had to take charge. "Who is it?" he asked with a posh English accent. He looked around before pointing the gun at the door, nodding at Mark. There was no answer, just the shuffling of feet. *Nothing.* And then someone threw a stone smashing the frosted front door's glass window. The glass clattered down, and a hand pushed through trying to fumble with the latch but the window was too high. Benazir looked at Mark. He nodded. "We have a gun and it's pointed right at the door."

"And we've been to Sainsbury's. Everything's free today. We have food and drinks. Hey Mark, let us come in."

"Oh, shit", Mark whispered. It's Ronald. You know him. He's an idiot. Fuck."

"Is he a friend of yours?" Benazir whispered back.

"Oh god, no. He's an asshole."

"What does he want here? "Benazir looked at his friend with his eyes widening.

"What d'you want, Ronald? I can't let you in. My mum's sick."

"Your mother? What is it?" This guy didn't give up. "Is it that bad?"

"Yeah. Sorry, mate."

"But we have food," Ronald whined.

"What are you doing out on the streets? It's bloody dangerous." Mark tried to keep the panic out of his voice.

"Not for me", Ronald laughed. "We're out hunting."

"Hunting what?"

"Muslims, mate. Muslims. Only wondered if you know where this dirty bastard lives. You know, the one who dared to go to our school."

"Sorry, I do not understand who you're talking about." *Shit.* "We have lots of Muslims in our school."

"That's it. That's why he's here. Because of me. He assumes you know my house", Benazir whispered, his face showing an unhealthy grey.

"Come on, you know. This lazy piece of crap. Wanted to become a Muslim priest or something like that. I saw you talking a lot."

"Oh, Ben."

"Yes, whatever his fucking name is."

"Sorry, I have no idea where he lives. I've never been there. We're not friends. We've just talked at school, mate." Benazir's life now depended on Mark. He would decide his future in the next few seconds.

"Who's in there with you? Ronald asked mistrusting. "It wasn't you who spoke earlier." Mark didn't like Ronald, and he could have done without all of it, but if he handed over Benazir and pretended to be Christian, maybe these guys would protect him. He was white. He felt weak in the legs and thought of his father and what he would have done. There was no question what his mother would have decided. But then he realised it didn't matter. "It's my cousin. He was meant to be here only for one night, but stayed when all this started. His parents haven't picked him up yet."

Mark could see, that one guy tried to climb up and peak through the little window. He couldn't be sure it was Ronald. He gestured to Benazir to hide in a corner so they couldn't see his friend. Benazir gave him the gun. He was still trembling, but this was now so familiar to him, that it almost seemed comforting. A second thought followed; it didn't matter if he died. Because what was there to come, anyway? Did anybody care if he was alive? He sank down in the corner Mark had pointed at? In his mind, he could see all the guys standing in front of the door. They wouldn't leave. They were here to have a party. He sat and watched Mark. And the boy raised the gun. "You better go now, Ronald." Tonight's not a good night for a party, and I don't know where Ben lives.

"Damn", Ronald moaned." Not guiltily, Benazir thought. He sounded as if he was a small boy whose toy had just been taken away.

"Okay," Mark answered, his voice only just above a whisper. Benazir felt the impulse to do something for him, but that was out of the question. All he wanted was to get home and spend time with Aisha. The boy was hoping she wouldn't cry, making Ronald ask even more questions. Ronald would and maybe even break the door. Benazir only wanted a few minutes' peace. The banging started again. This time it was laughter coming from all the other guys. Let's get in, Ro. We'll find this bastard another time, but we could have a party here.

"Sorry, mate. We can't leave," Ronald said. The answer was a single shot. Mark stood on a stool and had pointed the gun through the broken window. One scream. Silence. "Fuck." They couldn't be sure who said it. It wasn't Ronald. Mark couldn't bring himself to think about what he would find if he opened the door. He wasn't a killer. His dream was to be a doctor. He wanted to save people's lives. The boy's brain wouldn't allow him to think in too much detail about what he might have just done. He couldn't allow himself to assume he was a murderer. Ronald hadn't been killed. Mark clung to that thought. He wasn't dead. "Ronald?" He stood breathing, sobbing. They were tears of frustration, grief and anger, all mixed into one. Even if he lived a long life, he would never forget how he felt right now, the images in his head and the reality of what boys could do to other boys in a moment of madness. He stepped off the little stool, pushed it away and opened the door, still pointing the gun. There had to be another way. But he couldn't think of anything. He had to look and find out. Asking Benazir to do it would be too much of a risk. He pushed open the door further. If he had to shoot again, he would. Maybe it would drive him crazy later, but his self-preserving instincts were stronger. He had done it twice before and hadn't messed up. Well, it had been Benazir the first time, but it didn't matter. He would have done it. Something told him it might not be the last time. He would break every rule in the book. Mark peeked through the slightly open door. "Ronald?" No answer. The boy noticed some activity, but he couldn't be sure it came from the boys Ronald had arrived with. It sounded like someone was talking on the phone, to quick, messing up words. So, the line hadn't been cut off. There was a small spur of hope in his heart, and then he realised the television was still running. The only thing that hadn't stopped functioning yet was the water and the power. Well, at least something. This told him someone still had control somewhere. Mark looked down. And all hope was lost. Ronald was dead, his broken eyes staring up at the sky and his friends had run away just leaving him there. A few houses up, a woman emerged from her home, running away. Mark didn't want to know what was going on there. Mark called for Benazir. "Ben, they're gone, and Ronald is dead. Help me. We can't leave him here." His friend got up, and Mark allowed him to pass. "Shit." There was nothing else Benazir could say. "I know. But we have to get him off the porch. We don't want to draw attention to our house. We can't do anything for him. It's too late." They stumbled outside. "We must get him inside, Ben."

"Yep, just another one won't matter. "Benazir put a hand in front of his mouth when he realised what he had said. But Mark just started laughing hysterically. "Yep… ha, ha. That's right. We have quite a zombie party going on in there." It was wrong, but Benazir couldn't help himself smiling. When they had themselves under control they bend down, Benazir pulled Ronald's arms, and Mark picked up his legs. While doing that they looked around, realising all the broken bottles, rotting vegetables, sewage and other things in the middle of the road. "It's a mess. I have no idea how they will clean this up again." Mark looked at Benazir. "Maybe they won't."

"You know, what I just thought. This is only the beginning. The fighting in the streets has already started, soon they will burn the place down, and people are already being raped and killed. Nobody is in control. What has happened, Mark? I mean there should be soldiers by now. Where is the military? And look at the house over there. *Jesus Christ is the saviour. Muslims will burn in hell.* Mark, this is a religious war. Like in Sudan. My dad had told me how Christians killed the few Muslims living there." Mark just sighed. "Help me get Ronald inside. We're too exposed here." He tried to operate with sufficient thought and do what they required now. He would think about everything else later. Both boys realised that yesterday they had heard sirens the whole day and today there was nothing, just silence. Mark didn't want to think about fights or how they would survive. What they would eat when they ran out of food in the next few days and what it would mean if the water wouldn't work anymore. His hands were dirty, where he had touched the outside walls and his jeans had a hole, but he didn't care. He just wiped his palms down the front of his t-shirt and started to lift and push Ronald's body. The boy reached up and opened the door wider. Ben stumbled back, still pulling the boy's arms. Ronald's face was covered in blood. Mark's bullet had hit him in the forehead. Benazir couldn't stop staring at it. His breath sped up. How was it possible for a boy his age to be so heavy? Because he was dead? And why was Mark unfazed by all of this? Benazir's mind wandered, and he thought about his mother, who hadn't loved him. He realised Aisha would have no memories of her. And he didn't even pack a photograph. She would never know how her mother had looked like. She would know her mother only by stories her brother would tell her. And then it happened. He became angry. Furious. He didn't know why but while he was pulling Ronald's body inside the house the dam burst. He felt pure anger spreading through his body until he could only feel this sudden rage. He wrapped his hands around Ronald's wrists until they started to hurt and the blood rushed to his head. He didn't have to live like this and lose everybody he loved. He could fight back. It was time to stop being a boy. Time to forget his dream of becoming an Iman and to grow up.

Ross-on-Wye, Herefordshire

Five years later

The dreams he had were always the same. He raced forward. Glancing left and right. Running away. Staying away from the main roads. There were screams and footsteps behind him. Someone wanted him to stop to catch him. But it scared the man. He felt like a small boy. His mind was racing trying to work out where to run next. He ended up on a cul-de-sac, but there was fence he could climb. He attempted to black out everything - where he was running to, who was behind him, chasing him. All he wanted was to live, and his instinct and self-preservation took over. He could feel fear, but it didn't stop him from jumping the fence and running as fast as he could. Someone fired a shot at him, but he was ok. It didn't hit him. Someone screamed. He stumbled to the right, into another small street. He called for help, but there was nobody to help him. There were only the footsteps and some hard breathing behind him. The man's sides were burning. He wasn't sure how much longer he could run. He feared he would have to slow down soon. He looked everywhere for an escape route, an open gate, a house he could hide in, any escape from the yelling behind him. But he could find nothing. He didn't know what to do. The steps came closer. "Please, please leave me alone. Please." It was all he could think to say, and he hoped it would stop them, whoever they were. He started to slow down. He couldn't run like that much longer. And then he saw an open door. Only an open door but it looked like heaven. He ran into the house and slammed the door shut behind him. He locked it and slid down on the wall next to it, panting. He just sat there trying to get his breathing back and stared into the flames of a log fire that was burning right in front of him. He started praying. Praying for his safety, for not being killed tonight. There was silence, but then the knocking started. People were begging him to let them in. He didn't understand it. It didn't sound like they were trying to get to and hurt him. It sounded like these voices were begging for his help. Someone was screaming in pain. He stood up. He wrapped his arms around himself and didn't want to open the door, but somehow, he felt like he had to. He was alone and still so young. All he wanted was his mother. She would make sure he was safe. But she was dead. Huge tears welled up in his eyes. The ferocity of his response triggered alarm bells. Why did he know his mother was dead? And who were these people outside? Someone was crying outside now. And they were knocking again screaming for him to let him in and help. Finally, he could no longer bear it and opened the door. He didn't care anymore if they would kill him. He just wanted this nightmare to end. His eyes drifted to the huge group of people standing in front of the door. They were all strangers, but somehow, they looked familiar.

They were all injured or sick. There was blood dripping down their faces, their skin was hanging off, and their bodies were covered in large cancerous tumours. "Help us, please," they whispered. "We're not scavengers. Please. There are so many, many more of us and we all need your help. Maybe you could just help a few. We're dying." The boy stumbled back. It occurred to him he had no idea how to help these people even if he wanted to. "I'm not a doctor. I can't help you. Go somewhere else and leave me alone." Why did they assume everything was up to him? "You're almost a doctor. You always wanted to become a doctor. Don't you remember? Please, you must help us. One of the people, a man who had been standing right at the front took his arm. "Please." It started to pour, and the water rain splashed up on them washing off the blood. Their faces began to melt changing into something else. He could see his mother and his father, his old neighbours and friends, all of them dead now. He squatted and steadied his elbows on his knees. "I don't know what to do." His eyes were wide and his mouth hung open, but somehow it was a thrilling thought to be able to help, to help anybody. The idea hit him with a force that shook him to his core. He would learn to be a healer. He would help, and if he couldn't help these people, he would help others. He trembled and stretched out his arm towards his family, but they just disappeared.

"Dad? Dad?" He could feel someone shaking his arm. Sweat was running down his face. "Dad, you're dreaming again. You were screaming." The man opened his eyes and looked at his daughter. "I'm ok, pumpkin. It was just a dream. A nightmare, but just a dream." He could still feel the fierce flame of desire from deep within, the wish of bringing people back to life. And he remembered how people used to trust these things. Life after death. He remembered going to church with his parents when he was little and hearing about a place he hadn't known existed. A place his mother knew and told him about, something he could never imagine. He had listened to the message coming from someone called a minister, but he had never trusted it. And when everything had gone crazy, people who believed just seemed to confirm that nothing of it could be true. No-one was nice and spread love and tolerance. No, you had to belong to the right religious group, otherwise you were as good as dead and these people had called themselves Christians. They had complained about Muslims who just killed everybody, but they were no better themselves. There had been no escape, or so it had seemed. He had to learn quite a lot about medicine, healing people's bodies to a certain extent but he wished he could heal people's minds. He remembered when he was young and had to hide all the time. Him and other people who had been thrown in together by chance. They were just teenagers, but they had learned to look after themselves, always being alert. Their childhood had ended. It had been hard, but he remembers realising he was lucky he wasn't a girl. At least they didn't have to fight off men and boys trying to rape them. He looked at his daughter. She would have it so much harder unless she joined one of these religious cults. Back then he'd tried it, but it was not for him. They were all hypocrites. Some like him had joined to be protected and not have to fight every day, and most of the girls were with these groups because they didn't want to be raped. Well, that didn't protect them. The only difference was they were now being attacked daily by people they knew instead of strangers all in the name of cleansing their souls. Food was more and more difficult to find. Prayers didn't change that. So, he had embraced the forest, at least they could find something to eat there and could hide. Nobody would force them to watch things they didn't want to see. Also, his skills at hunting had grown. The forest had protected them. Soon they could provide enough meat even to have some for the winter. Whenever they had entered an empty house in the city, the man had taken some books he had found about how to conserve food and after trying it a couple of times it had worked. Their knowledge and skills grew until they would know just by a small sound whether they were approaching a deer, a cow that had run away, a squirrel in the trees or if they should hide because it was a bear or a wolf. He could look at a track and know which animal had made it or if it was a man and they should keep away. He even realised if the creature was running away from something or someone. And there were times when they almost had enjoyed themselves. Almost. On some days it was easy to forget what had been going on. They had survived the winter in the city and then it had been summer. I had taken them a long time to find the forest, and his daughter had grown into a toddler, but one day they had found it. And the forest had provided them with everything they needed, or so they had thought. But winter came. It always did. In the winter you couldn't just sleep on the floor only protected by a few leaves. When winter came, he had finally realised that nothing would ever be as it was before. "Dad?"

"Yes, pumpkin."

"What are you thinking?"

"I think we need to start dinner and build something to protect us from the rain. Winter will be here soon. And now we need breakfast for Sammy. Are you listening to me?"

The girl shrieked in delight. "Daddy. We don't need to feed him. He's feeding us." She pointed straight ahead. Sammy was just running towards them. His ears were flopping in the wind with delight, and his tail was wagging as if he had found the biggest threat in the world. And he had. He was carrying a huge pheasant in his snout. Well, it was probably average size, but to them, it looked huge. They hadn't seen a pheasant in a long while. He ran with his head up high and a bounce in his step. When he reached them, he just dropped the bird and looked at them. The girl padded his head. "Good boy. Good Sammy. You are such a good dog."

A gentle breeze caused the bushes to sway, and the man noticed it didn't smell of rain anymore. "Ok, let's make a fire then. I guess we will have pheasant for dinner. When the fire was burning, and the bird was simmering in a pot they had saved years ago, his mind wandered back again to the time when he had lived with all these people. There was no greater being. The man was sure. He shook his head. If there was, he wouldn't have allowed this. Not the fights and the explosions and the hunger. That was man-made. But the suffering of good people, the death of so many children. No god could want this. The man felt his heart race, memories of a whole lifetime. At least that's how it felt. Women and children, all dead. He looked up. The girl was playing with Sammy who was chewing on some pheasant meat. He needed to protect her. He needed to make sure she was safe before he would die. His friend had died just in an instant. He had tried to save him and almost succeeded. But how could they have been so different? They had been fighting together for such a long time, but his friend had always kept his faith. He had prayed every day even though it changed nothing. For the man's mate there had always been hope. But he would never see him again. And then the man realised they had been searching for years to find a place, but maybe there was nowhere to go to anymore. Maybe they had to build something new. Civilisations had always been born and died for thousands of years. He remembered how fascinated he had been by the Maya when he was a small child. But their great monuments and cities had just been swallowed by the South American jungles, the Indus Civilisation in India, Pakistan, Iran, Afghanistan with its grand walkways and brick hives of houses just abandoned thousands of years ago, the people of Easter Island, the Mississippians. None of them was saved, and they couldn't save themselves, so they just disappeared. Like all these cults that had sprung from nowhere during the last few years claiming to hold the truth, the only truth but just tried to control people. None of them would survive for a long time. They held nothing good, and people did always fight them. It didn't matter what truth they claimed to have, it didn't matter if it was a twisted version of something that already existed or a belief people had just made up. None of it held the answer. It was just for people who were lost and tried to cling on to something. People who needed something else than the everyday struggle for survival and the constant daily fret to their lives. He looked at the little girl. None of that would help them. They wouldn't find a place to stay unless they would build it themselves. He looked around. The forest was green and lush. It provided them with everything they needed. And there was not only food; it provided entertainment and herbs to heal the body and mind. Well, to a certain extent anyway. There was a river running just a few metres from where they were, Sammy could warn them if there was a stranger and provide them with the occasional pheasant, so they wouldn't have to waste precious bullets. He was tired of running away and not knowing what they were running towards. He still couldn't believe how long they had stayed in London. It was probably even more amazing that they had survived that long in a city. Any city. He had seen so many houses and their occupants that attackers had tried to burn. After a while, it didn't matter anymore. And hunger had always taken them by surprise even though after a while they should have got used to it, but they never did. They had never stayed in one place for long, and they ate what they could find as they walked, not caring about the sweet taste of some half rotten food. Contemplating about it, they were lucky they had never become ill apart from the occasional upset stomach. The hunger had been so intense that eating had made their bodies ache. But a bigger problem than finding food was getting access to clean water. When they couldn't find bottled water anymore or were being chased away, they had drunk from little ponds, springs and rivers not caring if it would be safe for them. Well, at that age he hadn't known a lot about contaminated water. At points, they drank from muddy puddles because they were so desperate, not even daring to make a fire. They had tried to stay away from people always being aware of men's voices nearby. Especially when they were loud and laughing. Big groups of three or more were the most dangerous. They felt safe in numbers and didn't mind killing boys. Boys couldn't be raped, and they were competition. They had always tried to keep inside of empty buildings and only left when they had to. But after a while they realised, they wouldn't survive on their own much longer, not in the city anyway. The man remembered the first time he had killed somebody. The memory still haunted him.

They had always been drifting, always prepared to defend themselves. And he remembered that he could never understand why people turned so violent for no reason. He could understand when they were fighting for food and water, but a lot of these people just killed each other for thinking a different way or looking different, too dark, too light, too small, too tall. Any reason was a good one to kill. Sometimes he felt like no normal human was being left. They never felt safe, always imagining someone to be after them, so they had just kept moving. In the beginning, they only tried to stay alive long enough until the government would restore order. But when they heard about the first mushroom cloud, they realised nobody would come and save them. They would just die together with everybody else. If nuclear bombs exploded, even if it was not near them yet, it could only mean one of two things. Either nobody controlled them anymore, and one by one they would explode eventually because there was no working security system anymore or people hated each other so much, that they would use anything against each other, not caring if this would kill the whole planet. He couldn't be sure but maybe that day had turned him into an atheist, the day he heard about the mushroom cloud. The day the American president and the North Korean ruler finally decided to used their weapons. That was when the man truly had become scared. Because what else was there to wait for. They had spent months trying to survive but what was the point? He shivered remembering these dark days.

The wind had grown slightly colder, and he looked at the girl wanting to tell her to put on another jumper as a protection against the wind. The cold was eating its way into his skin. The girl would be cold now.

19th of September 2021 London
Benazir and Mark

It had been hard work, but finally, they had pushed and pulled Ronald's body back into the house. For a second they both sat there panting, not looking at each other until Benazir got up and locked the door. "What if they come back?"

"Who?"

"His friends."

"I don't think they were his friends. He's not the person who has friends."

"I know. But still."

The saddest eyes Benazir had ever seen stared back at him from Mark's face. They were vast and haunted. He was only thirteen, but he looked older and too wise, too experienced. But Benazir probably didn't look any different. He'd tried his best to make sense of what had happened and what was still ahead of them. He remembered everything that they had seen today and realised they had stolen his childhood. As to the why, he couldn't come up with an answer. So, what would they do now? Sit here and wait with three dead people in the house?

"Do you know what I just thought about?" Benazir's head jerked up.

"What?"

"Well, I heard this story about a group of people whose plane crashed in the mountains somewhere. And after they ran out of food, they started to eat each other."

"Thanks, Mark. That helps. We will not eat dead people. Forget it. I rather starve."

"If you say so."

"Yes, I say so." Aisha started crying. "I need to feed her."

"She'll need more milk soon."

"Well, at least she won't eat body parts. "

It wasn't funny, but they suddenly burst out into laughter. "No, she has got no teeth yet." Benazir chuckled trying hard to calm down again. "Stop it. We owe them some respect." Mark tried to suppress a chuckle by pushing his lips together and finally succeeded. "We could bury them in the garden before they smell."

"Are you sure? I mean it's mainly your family. You should decide. But… Mark, I'm not sure how to say this nicely. Maybe it's better to burn them. You wouldn't want their bodies to be washed up again. I know little about burials. You know, how deep you should do it and I have heard about animals digging…." He turned his head to the TV. "See. It's not just here." There were reports about similar events from foreign correspondents in a lot of other countries. Buildings were on fire, and people chanted religious slogans while they were throwing stones and shooting others at the same time. There were thousands of deaths among the rioters in Europe, America, Afghanistan and Asia. The world had gone crazy and looked so similar everywhere. People were told to stay at home, and there were announcements of food rationing, which would make things worse. Police and military were on the streets trying to restore order, but they were outnumbered on a large scale. "I want my mum," Mark whispered.

"I do, mine I mean, but I guess we will not get what we want. See, I need to feed and change Aisha. I will be as quick as I can. Are you ok, down here?"

"What? Ehm… yes, sure." Benazir looked at his friend and frowned, but he had no choice and just walked upstairs to get his sister. Mark just kept staring at the TV watching the fires and the chanting. He listened to the words, not being entirely sure what they meant, but instinctively knowing that they wouldn't get out of this mess soon. And suddenly there was just a blank screen. "What happened?" Benazir shouted from upstairs, but he didn't wait for an answer from Mark. "Bugger. The power's gone."

It looks like you have to feed Aisha cold milk. Can you manage?"

"I guess so. I'm just glad this happened during the day."

"Ben?"

"Yes, I think there must be safety zones, somewhere."

"What?"

"Well, I mean. You know what they always show in movies when there's a disaster. They always try to save women and children. I mean we're in England, for god's sake. They won't let women and children starve." Outside the windows a quick flash and a boom could be heard. The boys flinched. Benazir closed his eyes. He was holding his sister who was now screaming her head off. "Ben… you need to change her. I don't want to draw attention." Mark lingered in the doorway while his friend followed his instructions. As soon as Aisha had a bottle in her mouth, she seemed happy. It didn't seem to matter that it was a cold formula. She looked greedy the way she was sucking, and Mark smiled. It felt wrong, but he couldn't help it. It was as if someone else, a different and quiet Mark had taken over his body and mind. Someone who could deal with whatever was to come. Benazir nodded at him "She'll be alright. Your mum has quite a few boxes of formula here in the kitchen."

"You know what this means, don't you?" Mark looked at him.

"What's that?"

"Well, we have to decide. Stay here with all the boxes of formula and the tinned food we've got, not knowing if we will be saved and hope nobody will try to break in again. Or we take as much as we can carry and get out. "

"Get out and do what? Go to a safety zone? Mark, they have said nothing about a safety zone on television."

"I know, but what else is there? This can take weeks if not even months. I mean, haven't you listened to the news? The same thing is going on everywhere in the world. There aren't enough military and police to keep order any more. Too many fights, fires, explosions. They're popping up everywhere. The police are trying to keep order but there's not enough staff. It's crazy. And being honest… I think the media reporting it, makes the whole thing worse. People starting to think they can do whatever they like. Remember the last few months? It got from bad to worse. We just didn't pay enough attention. You think it just kicked off yesterday? It hasn't. It just came to our homes today, but it has been happening for ages. And the military? They haven't managed a safe zone. I have heard nothing. They kept us in the dark."

"Maybe not right now, but I guess people will calm down if the military comes in with tanks and the Royal Air Force bombs them from planes."

"What?"

"Well, you know what I mean. Do you think the government or shall I say the governments will just watch and let people kill each other? They will put everything in the hands of the police but if that doesn't work… I mean think about it. There's much more at stake here than a few lives they don't care about. They can't allow terrorists, and I mean any terrorist, take control of nuclear power plants or even worse atomic weapons. Have you got any idea what that would mean? You've seen these crazy fundamentalists. They want to die. They think they die and go to heaven. One of them would push the button at some point. And then obviously countries have to think about smaller things like water, sewage. I mean diseases could come from that if it doesn't run properly. Maybe not straight away but after a couple of months or maybe even weeks, we would be back to the Middle Ages. So, in comparison killing a few looters with a bomb is a relatively small thing to do".

"Do you think it's already that bad?"

"Yes, I do. And as mad as it might sound, I think we're the safest here in the house. Yes, people can still try to break in, but there are so many houses on this street. If we're lucky, we might be one of the last ones these people try." Mark looked at him. "You might be right. I guess. But I cannot stay with these bodies."

"Well, let's bury them. Let's give your family the burial they deserve and let's think about the others later. Four people, well. Three. I'm not sure what we should do. Dig a grave? What do you do if you cannot call an Iman, I mean a funeral service?" Like a dreamy dancer waking up from performing a well-rehearsed move, Mark turned around. He just looked at Benazir. His body was rigid. "You know you're talking about my mum, my dad and my brother. They're the only family I have." He hesitates. "Had." Benazir's horror was instantaneous. "I'm sorry. I didn't mean… I just don't know what to do. Everything is so…"

"Messed up?" Mark smiled.

"There must be a stronger word. But messed up will do for now. I'm sorry. You didn't have time to say goodbye."

"That's the way it is at the moment. You couldn't say goodbye either."

"That's different."

"How."

"My father… never mind."

"Your father, what?"

"My father. He is… wasn't like yours."

"You mean because he was one of the suicide bombers?" Benazir's head jerked up. "You knew?"

"I have done nothing than watch television when it happened." Benazir looked at him and then turned away as if respecting Mark's privacy. "And you saw a picture of my dad. Hang on… you've never been at my house. How could you…?"

"He picked you up from school once or twice. His face was familiar and my father told me."

"You could inform the police."

"About what, that I knew your father?"

"No, that I'm hiding here at your house."

"I think you've done nothing wrong and we can't influence what our parents do. They made their own decisions… What I want to know is what you think."

"I don't know what I think. And if you want to go to the police now, I won't stop you. Tell me if that's what you want."

"The police has other things to worry about if there's still police and I guess there would be no point. Ben. I don't want to hand you over to the police or to anybody. You've done nothing wrong." Benazir's head felt empty. He didn't know what they should be doing. Mark sighed. "Let's look at the garden and see what we can do. We shouldn't leave it too long." For a moment Benazir didn't know what he was talking about, but then he clicked. "Are you sure?"

"Yes." He just followed Mark outside through the back door. Ironically, it was a bright day. A good day for a funeral, Benazir thought, smiling sadly. His eyes filled with tears and his hands clenched around his body as if holding it together. After a couple of deep breaths, Mark pointed at a corner. I know our garden is not big, but it's been enough so far."

"It's beautiful," Benazir mumbled.

"I think it's enough space for mum, dad and Brian over there." They looked around. No witnesses. The garden fence was high, and the bushes had grown to almost two-metres during the last few years. "I think there are shovels in the garden shed, and the ground is very soft. It shouldn't take too long, Ben." The boy just looked at him looking guilt stricken.

"Ben, we have to do this. There is no other way."

"How can you do that?"

"Do… what? Bury my family?"

"No, be so matter of fact. I don't know… just get on with it."

"You just got on with it. You just walked away."

"That's different."

"How's that different? And don't tell me because of what your father did."

"No, I have to take care of Aisha. You, well… you haven't got that."

"You mean, I have got nobody left?"

"Sorry."

"Ben, if I don't do this, I know I will break down. I will cry, and I don't know if I will ever be able to stop." Mark stretched a little and took a deep breath walking towards the garden shed.

He had been right. Digging three graves had just taken them something over two hours. The ground was soft, and there were no stones or other obstacles. "My mum just had it all refilled with new soil", Mark had said during one of the very short breaks they had taken. They could still hear the distant breaking of glass and the cheerful delight from gangs of teenagers, sometimes mixed with screams of their victims. But they tried to ignore it getting on with their task. It was too far away at the moment for them to worry about it too much. To move the bodies out of the house with dignity was far more important for now. They started with Brian, Mark's younger brother. Mark couldn't bear to look at him, so they covered the body with a blanket first. The next one was his mother. This was much harder as it felt like she weighed a ton. The last one was his father. This one was the most difficult, not because he was the heaviest out of all of them which he was - but because Mark broke down. He obviously couldn't take it anymore. He refused to carry him outside and just sobbed over the body for what felt like hours. Well, at least for Benazir. "Mark. Please. Mark. We have to do this. Say goodbye." But Mark didn't react, so Benazir just knelt beside them the palms of his hands turned towards his own face almost touching it. He closed his eyes and muttered a prayer into his hands. Mark wanted to yell for him to just shut up with his goddamn prayers. But he realised that Benazir didn't do it to hurt him. He truly trusted god and thought it would help his family enter paradise. He just looked at Benazir after he had finished. "Thanks. I don't think it will help, but thanks."

"It might not, but it does no harm," Benazir said, his lips pressed tightly together forcing them into a smile. It was midday already, and the air was saturated with the scents of dead people. "Let's do it," Mark said dryly. The dread he felt, contemplating about what was ahead of them, filled him with a kind of anxiety, an embrace that made his heart beat quicker. I would hurt. Nothing good would come of it. There was no heaven. It would only get worse from here.

"Mark?"

"What?"

"Come on. We need to do this if you want to get it done today."

"I'm wondering if we should do it. Maybe we could wait, and we could call the authorities and have a proper funeral when things get back to normal."

"Mark." Benazir put a hand on his shoulder. I understand you. I do, but we don't know when things will become normal again or if they ever do and bodies will… start… you know… stink." Mark forced a brief laugh. It seemed completely out of place, but he couldn't help it. "Do you accept such things, you know, a higher power?" Benazir shrugged. "I don't know. I can't say I do and I can't say I don't. Not anymore. I'm not sure. But it seems comforting. It's nice to think there is something or someone beyond explaining."

"Like what?"

"Possibilities, you know. That we will see our family again and all the people we loved and liked. The thought someone is watching and will not let us mess things up even more." Mark smiled. "Yes, I guess I know what you mean. It's a nice thought."

"You know what I mean? I guess… well I believe. I grew up being a believer. My parents taught me. I read the Quran regularly. But what my father did… I don't know."

"Let's do it", Mark just answered and stood up. Benazir sighed. This wouldn't be easy. The body just laid there with its arms and legs thrown out from his body. Benazir looked around once more. He could feel his stomach playing up and wasn't sure anymore if he could do this. But he had to. He needed to be the stronger one here. He placed the man's arms on his middle section and just looked at Mark. He nodded. They picked him up and carried him outside into the garden. Mark's father was heavier than they had thought. He had been a big man, and now he was a dead weight. Benazir was panting from the exertion of carrying someone twice his weight and they were dragging him more than anything. But he tried not to think about it. It would be ten times worse for Mark, seeing his father like that. Mark panted loudly as if trying to cover the sound of his dad's body being knocked against the furniture. Benazir's arms started to feel numb, and sweat was pouring down his back when they finally reached the man's resting place. They pushed him near the hole they had dug, none of them wanting to spend more time contemplating about it. They grew quiet just staring at it. Carrying Mark's dad outside had proofed to be the most difficult thing they had ever done in their entire life, but they had managed. Now they just stood there, panting, looking at the three bodies covered by blankets. Mark's face had a grave expression. "I guess if we must, then we must." He fell silent. Tears were running down his face – finally. "I don't know what to do now. I've never arranged a funeral."

"Guess we have to… well… put… them into the… grave. You know what I mean."

"Yes. I know. Ok."

"Shall we have a break? "Benazir asked. Mark hesitated. "No… no. I think not. Let's just do it." They went on their knees and started shuffling the bodies down the hole. They just sat there watching it for a while.

"Maybe, you want to say a few words. You know about their lives." Benazir breathed.

"No, that would be… I don't know weird. I don't think they can hear it and… no. I would just like to think for a moment. But we need to cover them. Here, use the shuffle." Covering them was not as hard as Mark thought it would be. It gave them something to do, something physical which felt good. It took his mind of what happened in the last two days. But it didn't last long. He threw the last pieces of earth on the grave of his family with his bare hands. It didn't make any difference. They were still dead. "Do you want to put some flowers on it? There are enough here in the garden. I could get them."

"I guess so."

Benazir got up. He was glad he could do something. His tears came suddenly like a summer shower. He turned around so Mark couldn't see him. He wept for his mum and his dad and the fact that he felt like they never really loved him. It should make it easier to lose them, but somehow it didn't. But he couldn't change it and just bend down picking some yellow daisies. He turned around, walked back and put them on the grave of Mark's family. His friend didn't move. "Mark, we need to think about what we want to do with the other bodies in the house.

"What?"

"You know, Ronald, the paramedic and the policeman."

"We cannot bury them with my parents and maybe someone will come looking for them."

"I know, it's not a nice thought. But they wouldn't be in the same place, just the same garden. If we will stay in the house for a while, we can't do it with dead bodies. I don't think anybody search for them." There was something strange about Benazir. His body didn't move, and his voice sounded flat. His short black hair gave the impression of someone straight out of a zombie movie. "I know Benazir and I think you need a break. You don't... look... well."

"I'm ok."

"No, you're not. I think you're having a breakdown. Go somewhere to relax. Don't worry about me. Have a glass of water."

"The water doesn't work."

"What?"

"Seems like they switched it off. Why didn't you fill the bathtub and sinks when you still had the change?"

Mark hesitated for a second. "I didn't think." He sighed. And I guess neither of them did either." He shrugged. I think mum didn't' think it would come to this. And she had other things to worry about, once dad was.... you know."

His friend just looked at him and his gaze softened. "I wouldn't have thought about it either."

Mark tried to smile. "Don't worry. We have lots of bottled water in the kitchen. Use that. And have a look at your sister. I'm sure she's fine. I haven't heard her, but just in case." Benazir nodded and walked inside. A few moments later he came out with Aisha in his arms. "I'm sorry."

"What d'you mean? Is she alright?"

"Yes, it's just I cannot stay inside with all these..."

"I know."

"But they're here. I mean I can't see them, but I know they're here."

Mark just sighed. "It still feels better out here." There was just silence for a moment. Nothing interrupted it apart from the singing of some birds. "I guess we have to bury the other bodies, Ben." He held out his hand. "Come on." They walked in silence to the back door, lost in their thoughts and worries. When the almost reached it, they jumped back. A big bang hit their eardrums. "What the hell…" Mark shouted.

"I'm not sure. It sounded like an explosion." They had instinctively ducked, and Mark tried to look through the back window, but he couldn't see anything. It almost looked like there was smoke in the house but that couldn't be. Nothing was working. They couldn't have started a fire accidently. "Aish..", he turned to Benazir. But his friend was holding his sister in his arms. "We have to find out what it was."

"Maybe something broke."

"Broke? What?"

"I don't know a picture has fallen off the wall or something."

Mark shook his head. "No, it sounded like an explosion. Maybe gas?"

"I thought someone had turned the gas off."

"I thought so too, but maybe we were wrong." Mark realised his hands were trembling. He straightened up after a second trying to peak through the window again. It still looked hazy inside. But maybe it was just his mind playing tricks on him. He could feel the warm rays of the evening sun on his face. He said nothing because he wasn't sure what to do. But they couldn't stay out here forever. The silence between them started to make them feel awkward. And suddenly they could detect it - fire. "Oh, my goodness," Benazir whispered.

"What is it?"

"Can't you smell it. The house is on fire."

"But it can't be. Nothing…"

"Nothing's working. I know."

"I don't think it was an accident."

"What?"

"I think these idiots came back."

"I have no idea what you're talking about."

"His friends, Ronald's friends."

"I think they haven't realised we're in the garden. And they came back and tried to burn down the house."

"Are you sure? I mean, they can't do that. All my stuff is in there. All our stuff."

"No, I'm not sure. I have not heard or seen them. But the house is burning, and I just suspect it was them."

"We have to get inside."

"We can't."

"We have to," Mark was shouting now. "Where else can we go. There is nowhere we can go. We have no food or water." He put his hand on the door handle and started pulling it. "Mark don't," Benazir shouted. It was too late. The door opened, and a huge fireball threw both of them back outside. The impact was so unexpected and strong that there was no resistance from any of them. Flames continued to fly out the door, but the force of the fire fuelled by oxygen had just lasted for a second. Mark pushed himself up looking around in a daze. "We're fucked," he muttered. "Benazir." He turned to the side. His friend was just laying there. His clothes were scorched but not burned, and his face was black. "Ben," he screamed.

Ross-on-Wye, Herefordshire

Five years later

When he finally found her, he didn't have to worry. The girl had just turned and walked away with Sammy, finding more berries and completely forgetting to stay close. After watching her for a while, the man just said, "I think we should stay, pumpkin." The girl stopped and stood still for a moment, just looking at her father. She gazed around and bent down to Sammy, stroking him and tickling his ear. She ran her hands through his fur and looked straight into his eyes. The dog just sat there obediently. "What do you think, Sammy? Shall we stay? I mean here, right here?" Sammy cocked his head and barked. Only once, wagging his tail at the same time. The man still stood there, waiting but he couldn't help himself smiling. So, now they were at a point when they would listen to a dog's opinion. Well, it couldn't get much worse really, anyway. So, why not? "What did he say?" The girl wrapped her arms more tightly around Sammy, pressed her face into his fur and took a deep breath in. "He said yes. But I assume you think that's stupid.

A dog can't talk. But I think he wants to stay. "Are you sure?"

"Of, course I am. He told me in his doggy language."

"Well, if he wants to stay he probably has an excellent reason, and that's just how it is." They stood still, both smiling and feeling like they finally stopped running away. It was a deceptive belief. The man knew that. But for now, they didn't care. The dog, Sammy, barked again, jumping up and down as if he understood what they had said. "So, well I guess we need to build a place where we are safe and can put down our heads at night."

"Yes, something safe, where no-one can just come in. Something like a castle or something underground like a hobbit. The story you are always telling me. Yes, it would be nice to be a hobbit." The man laughed. Yes, that would be nice, wouldn't it? But it's dark underground, so we would need good eyes. "

"No, we just need a good nose like Sammy, and we would just need to sleep there. I mean during the day; we could be outside. I'd like to be somewhere safe when we sleep." The man frowned. This wasn't just funny fairy tale chit-chat anymore. It had given him an idea. A place underground, where nobody would know they were there. He started walking around digging little holes with his foot here and there. Sammy assumed it was a new game, and he started digging as well. The girl giggled. "Dad, what are you doing?" The man laughed. I'm trying to dig to China. "No, dad. That will take you ages", she giggled some more.

"You want to know what I'm doing. Well, you know that the earth is round, right?"

"Right."

"And you know, that as closer you get to the centre as hotter it gets. Well, I think if we dig deep enough, and I don't mean to China, I mean just a few metres down we discover that temperatures are always moderate in the winter and also in summer because the earth's temperature does not change much over the course of a year. We can use it as a natural source of energy, sheltering us from the elements, and…"

"And… nobody would know we're there", the girl added excitedly.

"Yes, I know for sure it's possible to build homes that are partially or almost completely buried beneath the ground because people have done it before. You know, long before everything collapsed. It wasn't very common when I grew up, but these houses have been around for a while. I read a book once when I was nine or ten about this family living in the 1970s, who feared the Russians and tried to reduce their dependence on oil, and apparently, they pulled it off. Ok, they build some bunker but it was in the ground and when I was a small child, a lot of people thought underground living was a great alternative and looked for ways to make it affordable and efficient."

"Dad?"

"Yes."

"What's affordable?"

"Well, it means you have enough money to buy something." The girl looked at him not understanding what he meant. "Oh, yes right. You probably don't know what money is. Well, I think I could explain that to you later. It will take a while. Anyway, these underground houses they've built didn't always work but often they did. What's important is that the material we'll use to build absorbs and keeps heat, and the best for that is earth. You know mud. It's impressive how long it can hold the temperature. Well, some of these houses I'm talking about weren't completely underground but above ground, but piles of soil are then pushed up against walls, all the way to the top to form protection of earth and vegetation that will separate the outside of the home from the open air. They build all the rooms in such a house beneath the surface of the earth and have an entrance from above ground. A short flight of stairs down is all that is necessary to reach the bottom of the home, as the underground rooms are only a few metres beneath the earth's surface because the temperatures are steady beyond this point." He had talked quicker and quicker, smiling, building a picture in his mind not realising that his girl was too young to understand. "Because it's below ground, it delivers the greatest amount of protection from high winds, thunderstorms, tornadoes, hurricanes, wildfires and bad people. However, because it is a hole in the ground, it can easily fill with snow or rainwater, and because the living areas are entirely beneath ground level, the sun cannot enter. We would need something to make sure the earth does not collapse over our heads. So, we need to find wood to build a proper roof, and we need some drainage or filtration to make sure that any moisture that comes from above can get away. And we need something so that water cannot work its way into our home from below. I can make our roof of soil and vegetation so that the roots of the plants will absorb the rain. Maybe we can build on a little hill like the one over there." He pointed ahead of him. "I guess we can't build like these people in my book because we haven't got a lot of the stuff they had but digging a hole and building a roof from wood should be possible. I'm sure I can do that. I can build wooden support for the walls. It will require little maintenance and can last for decades."

"Yes", the girl shouted, excitedly. "I'll help you."

"Alright then. Let's have a look at the hill and see if we can start building a home. "

One year later

The small wooden table was set against the wall of the house, and a candle was lighting up the room. Well, technically it wasn't really a table. It was a tree stump which they had found ages ago and dragged into the house. But it was big enough to serve the purpose. The man and his little girl were sitting on boxes that functioned as stools digging into a simple vegetable stew. The girl was holding a plastic cup in her hand. "It's delicious," the man said. You have improved. I like it."

"It even has carrots in it. Can you see it?"

"Yes, it's perfect. I didn't know we had carrots."

"Yes, I found some last year and tried to multiply them, and it worked. We have lots at the back. "The man laughed. You mean in the ground."

"Yes, you know what I mean. And Sammy has caught more wild turkeys. He's getting superb. The foxes fear him as well." She giggled.

The man leaned back and studied her—here sitting underground in a hole, life was almost perfect. It had been over a year since they had to fight for food daily. Nobody had found them. And they had more than they could eat. They were getting stronger and the girl looked radiant and healthy. Sure, they still had to work hard, but they could see results. This winter would be the first time they didn't have to worry. They got a bit careless. To begin with, they had been watching every one of their steps but in the last few months… well, some peace had come over them. Maybe most people were dead and the rest… maybe they, too, just wanted to live and not being bothered. And when they ran out he still had bullets to shoot deer. He'd just done it once so far, and they still had lots of dried meat. He had been creeping through the woods until he had come across the big stud and with one shot he had taken him down. Their little house was well hidden underground, no-one had found them or destroyed it. It was almost shocking how long they hadn't seen people. Sure, they were in the middle of the woods but still; they had been lucky. The door was right at the front. They had found an old wooden panel, but they covered it in branches and leaves. They had to lift it up to get in but unless you knew you could not see it. Building this place had been a blessing. If they would continue to do as well, they might even have chickens. Well, the little girl wanted to have some, but they couldn't. They might draw attention. He still looked at the girl smiling. "Dad?"

"Yes, what is it pumpkin?"

"D'you know that herbal book you have."

"Yes."

"Maybe I should start reading it. You know. I could learn about all the vegetables."

"Well, you're more than welcome, but the book explains nothing about vegetables, just herbs and even there it's just for medical purposes not for food."

"Oh. Ah, well that doesn't matter. I can still learn about them. I can go out with Sammy and pick some and then I can just compare it to the ones in the book. Couldn't I?"

"Of course, you could. But you know I don't want you to go too far away from the house without me."

"I know, but it's boring always staying inside."

"You don't stay inside all the time, pumpkin."

"We're outside all the time." Several thoughts hit him. First, it almost made him happy that she seemed to be bored. He never thought this day would come. It was a sign that maybe things would become quieter. And secondly maybe giving her the book was not a bad idea. There would never be a school for her, but she should learn as much as possible, especially things that could ensure her survival. Now, how to bring it about? He could read things out to her, explain them and go to the forest with her or he could let her explore on her own. After all, they hadn't seen people for over a year now. Maybe most of them were dead, killed by nuclear weapons or other illnesses. Whatever it was, they shouldn't waste time sitting here. He got up and took the book from one of the wonky shelves he had made months ago. The girl sat on his lap, and they were flipping through the photographs with an explanation for all the herbs. Finally, the girl lifted her gaze and pointed at a plant. "I know this one. I've seen it before. It smells nice. What's it called? She moved her fingers along the letters. P-E-P-P-E-R-M-I-N-T. Peppermint oil has been used for a variety of problems such as irrit… irritab…" She sighed. "Irritable bowel syndrome." The man said.

"Yes, and indigestion, heartburn, nausea, colds… Oh, I have had lots of colds. I could have used it."

"You did. I made peppermint tea for you lots of time."

"Really. I don't remember."

"Well, you probably couldn't smell it because your nose was blocked, but I did."

"You know what."

"What?"

"We should find some, and then I will dry it and put it in the book next to the picture."

"That will be exhausting. Have you got any idea how many herbs there are? You won't be able to sleep." She laughed. "I will just doze. But dad, I don't mean collecting it all today. I mean we could start and collect one every day or so." He smiled at her, got up and went to the little hole serving as a window, holding his face to the breeze, inhaling the scent of the damp house, its walls and the forest smell drifting through the air. He looked at her beautiful face and saw the excitement of a little seven-year-old girl showing in her eyes. The loneliness and longing for a life free of fear was not showing anymore. She was just a little girl getting excited about the possibilities. "Ok, darling. But take Sammy and don't walk to far away. If you hear or see anything strange come back." He hadn't even finished when the girl was already hanging around his neck, just shouting: "Thank you, thank you, thank you." She ran out and almost lost her balance when stumbling into the blinding sun outside. Sammy broke in excitement and the man couldn't help but grin widely. It felt strange on his face. He could feel a twinge of worry in his stomach and suddenly he wasn't sure anymore if he had made the right decision. They didn't know who was out there. Sure, they had seen nobody for a long while but that could have been a coincidence. And even if there weren't any men hiding in the forest, there were still wild animals. Not being disturbed by humans during the last few years had increased their appearances. The man hadn't seen one, but he was certain he had heard a wolf's howling a few days ago. This wasn't a playground. It was a forest and an unknown one for them. The man was suddenly sure they hadn't seen the worst yet. His stomach was twisted in knots. He trudged back to the table and put away the self-made cutlery. No, he couldn't leave her there on her own even with Sammy. He had proven to be a real protective dog but a bear could easily kill him. Ha sat down, got up again, sat down and stormed out of the house, almost falling over his own feet. He had to find her. He didn't even bother to put on a jacket. His hands pushed away the branches. For one moment he turned around to look at the house. It was well hidden. Unless you walked very close, you couldn't see there was a house hidden in the ground. His heart was thumping so hard that he was sure he would have a heart attack if he couldn't find her soon. He hoped he could trust her to find her way around, well until he found her, anyway. She had to—she had no choice. And then he could hear Sammy barking. It was not a fun bark, not like the one earlier when the dog had been excited to go out. It was a bark followed by a growl. A threatening growl. The man felt like time was running out and ran quicker. And then he saw her. His little pumpkin stood with her back to him, almost leaning against a big oak tree, trying to walk backwards.

Sammy was standing right in front of her in a defensive pose. A man stood in front of them smiling, but it didn't look friendly. He had planted his legs firmly apart, standing straight and holding a baseball bat, moving it from one hand to another. He had not taken care of his beard for years. It had just been growing and made him look even more threatening. He was muscled and didn't look starved. He had found food and feed himself well. "Are you alone, darling," he asked sweetly, slapping the baseball bat into the palm of his right hand. Something was going on. But what was this guy planning? The man shook his head. "Don't worry, I will do nothing to you. I mean you have some great protection there, darling. What's his name? "The girl's father could see that this man was nervous, twitchy. "Where's your mummy? Can I talk to her?"

"No", the girls answered with a high voice. I haven't got a mummy, but you can talk to my daddy."

"Your daddy? "The man pulled each word like chewing gum. He glanced over his shoulder at the forest as if he was expecting someone else to appear. "Where's your daddy? He shouldn't leave you out here all on your own. Are you sure you have a daddy?"

"Yes, I have a daddy. What are you doing here?" The man stepped forward, Sammy growled louder and moved towards him, his head moving lower. The man stepped back. But he still looked like he had some ownership over the woods. He looked wary, but he didn't seem exactly scared. More like he weighed up his options. Maybe he was just trying to find a way around Sammy so he could do anything he wanted to the little girl. Anything. There were no police. Nobody knew they were here. All that was in his way was Sammy. But the dog stood his ground not moving one inch.

"Well."

"Well, what?"

"Do you want to speak to my daddy? He might be able to help you if you're hurt."

"What makes you think I'm hurt?"

"The blood." She pointed at him.

Her dad was just as surprised to hear this as the other man was. They both absorbed what the girl had just said for a moment. "Oh, yes. Sure. I'm not hurt badly," the man said. It's just a wound that doesn't seem to heal."

"What sort of wound?" the girl inquired. The man took a deep breath. "Well, just some tumour."

"Have you got cancer?" The man didn't answer straight away. The girl continued. "Did you get it because of the radiation?"

"You know about the radiation?"

"Yes, my dad told me about it. But I'm still not sure what it is. Why did it happen?"

"I guess people just messed it up. And maybe there was a higher power?"

"A higher power? From where? The power plants?"

The man laughed, and even her father smiled, who was still hiding in the bushes.

"No, I mean a higher power like a god, the Lord. Maybe he thought this planet would be much better off without people on it?"

"You mean someone powerful made these explosions happen?"

"Yes, maybe it was just time for a new start. Maybe our time was done." His words hung in the moist forest air, bouncing off the rocks and trees.

"But we are still here," the girl whispered." Maybe it wasn't our time." The man frowned. "What are you saying, Angel? Don't you trust the Lord."

"I'm not sure. Guess not. Haven't seen him." The frown on the man's forehead deepened. "I guess you're not…"

"I'm not what?"

"You looked like an angel. Here, in the middle of the woods. I thought it was a sign. That you were some… messiah. I thought you could heal me. Make everything… better. I guess I was wrong… I guess…" The man shot back, then lunged towards the girl, his face a mask of pain and fury, his hands outstretched. "Help me!" He crouched down and jumped, pushing away Sammy at the same time who was too surprised to react, gripping the girl's right forearm, yanking it up and twisting it and finally released it. The girl cried out in pain. By now Sammy forced his teeth into the man's arm, right where the bleeding wound seemed to be. The man screamed and let go of the girl. "Help me". He screamed: "Please help me. I can't live like this anymore", while kicking his feet into the dog's flanks, but

Sammy didn't let go. The girl's father had jumped out of the bush jamming his heel into the man's back. The man fell forward, his head smashing into the ground. The girl's dad grabbed the man's neck from behind. He tried to fight him off, turned and crashed his right fist into the father's stomach, but the punch was too weak. It didn't have any effect. Desperately he tried to grab the girl's father. But he lurched to his right, pushing the man back to the ground, his legs scratching the mud trying to find some support, his face rubbing the dirt, making him struggling for breath and starting to cough. In the last attempt, he grabbed the father's wrist, bend it and trying to twisting it in one great attempt. The girl's father shouted at him to let go, or he would break his neck. The man collapsed giving up. The girl's father gasped, getting up, just looking at the maniacs back. "Stay. Don't move."

It was over.

"If you move or just make a sound, I'll kill you!"

"Ok, mate. I trust you. I won't", he whispered, terrified. The girl's father grabbed the man by the cloth of his jacket, turning him around. He was now laying on his back, still panting heavily, holding his arm in agony. For a moment they just stared at each other. Sammy had let go of the man's arm, but he was still growling. "Sammy, it's ok." The girl's thin voice had the desired effect, and the dog stopped, walked over to her and laid down by her side. "Good boy." She patted him. "Are you ok, pumpkin?" the man asked sounding like he was at the edge of hysteria. "Yes, I'm fine. Dad, what did he mean by messiah?"

"Don't worry. It's a fairy tale. People just sometimes believe in fairy tales."

"It's not a fairy tale", the man on the ground whispered. "It can't be." He pulled himself up into a sitting position, putting his hands out. "No harm, I mean no harm. I just lost it. Didn't want to hurt your little girl. Didn't. ". He shifted his weight, trying to get more comfortable and pulled his legs in. "How bad is it?" the girls' father scowled at him. The man said nothing and just pulled up his sleeve. The wound was deep and oozing. It wasn't a normal cut. The infection had already spread. "It's not the only one. I have them everywhere. He closed his eyes and opened them again. "I don't want to die. I just want it to stop.

"Let me have a closer look." The man's father bent down. "I can't heal you. You know that, but maybe I can do something about the pain. Make it a little more bearable. But I cannot change what it is."

"Maybe we can pray together."

"We don't…"

"I know, you don't trust the Lord, but how can you be sure?" He just sighed, and his head fell to his chest.

"Maybe," the girl said. The man's hand went limp. He had no strength left. Sammy had walked towards him and was now sniffing at the wound. The man winced; his neck arched. He was traumatised, and he had just attacked the little girl, but how dangerous was he? They couldn't just let him lay here, but he couldn't walk. Or could he? It was a risk to bring him back to their little hideout. And how much of a fanatic was he?

19th of September 2021 London
Benazir and Mark

Mark threw himself at the boy, grabbing his shirt with both hands, shouting and sobbing, pulling his friends closer to him. Mark held on to Benazir's clothing and didn't say a word. He was just screaming. He took his jacket off and wrapped it around his friend in the fire's glow not realising his home was burning down to the ground. His cries mixed with Aisha's but he didn't hear her, and the baby girl eventual cried herself to sleep. It didn't bother him. All he wanted was for Benazir to wake up. After what felt like hours but judging by the house still burning, it couldn't have been longer than half hour Benazir stirred. Guttural sounds escaped his throat. He was in pain, but could move. "Ben, Ben, are you ok. Ben say something." He put some water on the boy's lips. The only bottle he had saved from the house, being aware enough to take it before they started digging the graves in the garden. To start with Benazir only moaned and didn't drink but then he lifted his head, and his lips drank greedily. Little by little, the boy came out of the cloud he was in. He was having a tough time. Almost every move seemed to hurt him. The reality of what his life had been just a few days ago to what it was now so sudden seemed to refrain him from coming back to reality. It almost seemed like he wanted to stay dazed and confused, dominated by memory loss and insanity. The past was the one thing Benazir was familiar with and trusted. He was thankful for having been able to live with a mum, a dad and a sister. He had nothing left now. "Mum," he moaned. Mark appreciated how he felt and said nothing. He had to come back on his own. Still, Mark's sadness would not go away and neither would Benazir's. Mark watched his friend, and he seethed with anger thinking of all the senseless killing, the murder of his parents and Benazir's family, how Ronald had tried to kill Benazir and for what? And how his friends had taken away the only hope they've had. He wanted to punish them, make them pay for what they'd done to him and Benazir. But he couldn't think of anything to do except to find them and repeat their violent act. Kill them. Find them and kill them, shoot them or knife them to death. They deserved it. Mark stared at Benazir. "We have to leave. You know that. If you don't do it for yourself or me, do it for Aisha." Benazir looked uneasy and turned to Mark. "And then? Where do we go?"

"We look for shelter. England's a war zone. There will be shelter somewhere. They do that in all war zones. Benazir swung his gaze over to Aisha. "And what about her?"

"We take her, of course. What did you think?"

"We haven't got nappies or formula. What happens until we find shelter, if we ever find anything."

"We can't stay here."

"Dammit, Mark. I know that. What happens if we cannot find the formula?" Benazir came unhinged.

"Are you scared?", Mark asked, smiling. It seemed wrong, but Benazir understood why he was doing it. Crying was not an option. His friend was barely keeping a lid on his anger. "Isn't that reason enough? We can't stay here."

"Those little bastards won't be punished," Benazir whispered.

"They might already be dead."

Benazir tried to get up and sank back on the grass moaning in pain. "Mark, I don't think I can get up."

"I'll help you. I don't think you've broken anything. Maybe you're burned a bit, but it's nothing serious. I'll help you. Come here. I think shock just intensifies the pain."

"Isn't it normally the other way around? You can't feel pain because the shock numbs it?"

"I'm not sure. Whatever. We have to get away from here. The house is burning to the ground," Mark said calmly, but his breathing accelerated.

"There's just evil everywhere, Mark. Maybe we should have burned in the house."

"Maybe we should've, but we haven't and we have to survive, even if it's just for Aisha."

"What future does she have?"

"It doesn't matter. We cannot choose for her. She has to do it for herself. She has to be able to choose to live or to die." Benazir smiled. And for the first time, it seemed to be genuine. "You're right; we need to give her a chance to decide. We have to live until she's old enough and maybe there's hope. For her I mean. But she's a girl. Won't it be even harder for her than it is for us when she grows up?"

"I don't know. Maybe it will be easier because she won't know any different. I mean the life how we know it is gone, right? Our families are dead. All we have left is our life. And it looks like it will be pretty shit. Our families are dead. Our house burned down."

"Your house has burned down."

"It's your house now just as much as it's mine. Things have changed."

"It's no-one's house then because it's just burning to the ground." Benazir smiled.

"Why does it matter? Someone would have broken in. All we have now is this." Mark held out his hand and showed Benazir the gun.

"You still got it. Wow. You're a genius."

"Well, whatever. The cartridge clip is locked into place, and it's almost fully loaded."

"It's yours. You carry it," Benazir said. "And put it somewhere where people cannot see it straight away. Make sure you can get to it quick, though. With the slightest squeeze of your finger, you need to be able to shoot someone. It's hard. This thing seems to come alive when you fire it, and it moves, you don't realise until you use it. It's easier to shoot, to commit a crime. It makes you feel strong, especially when you're sharing the streets with maniacs."

"I know. I shot before." Mark looked at Benazir. He just bit his lip. "Let's go."

Minutes later Benazir turned around when they reach the street, holding on tight to Aisha but Mark just kept walking, his lips closed. They kept close to the dark walls of the houses, ducked low, trying to keep away from people, staying away from lights. They didn't talk much. Benazir whispered: "Where are we going?"

"Somewhere safe, where we can find baby food for Aisha." They would head off into dangerous areas, people would try to kill them for no other reasons than their looks, but there was no choice. They couldn't go into hiding without milk for Benazir's sister. By now she had even stopped whimpering. They hadn't heard her cry for a long time. Somehow it made sense to find someone to help them. They didn't need to talk to know they were in deep troubles and talking about it would hurt them even more. All they wanted was to look away and not think about what was coming. They could see lights in front of them or on the side, the glow reflecting in puddles. But they never tried to see and find out where it came from. All the realised was that the power had come back on in areas. But what did it mean? Maybe the lights were just created by generators. Mark was frowning, and his face glistened with sweat. He felt tired. He was tall for his age, even though not formed like a grown man yet. His face still looked boyish because he was as old as he was. But one could see he would be a strong man one day if he survived. In those few hours, the roads were packed with people confused not knowing where to go trying to run away from the bad guys. But somehow someone always had an idea or heard of someone who had found out about a camp or a religious group that would save them. Most of the time there was no truth in it. But people were still hoping. They carried everything they owned, even wearing hats and goggles, preparing for the winter that was still not here, some of them too exhausted to walk any further, sitting on their dirty possessions by the side of the road like survivors of war. And they probably were. Their eyes were dark in their skulls. Frightened frames of men and women like migrants in their own country. The frailty of everything around them didn't escape the boy's notice. Every so often they got up and followed another group hoping their rumours would be true. It all looked hopeless. "Look around you", Benazir said. We've been walking for such a long time now. There's no camp."

"Maybe not a camp. But the police and the military don't just disappear. There must be a plan somewhere. If it works out in the long run who knows. But they will do something. They cannot risk for the world to go up in ash. Not if they can prevent it. Even if it means going in with tanks and killing their citizens. I think if we stay peaceful there's a chance. But Benazir knew what he knew. Time was running out for them and Aisha. They sat down by a brown wooden door in the grey shadows of an abandoned house just watching people walk by talking, throwing away their old read newspapers all the while Aisha slept. They could see her little chest move up and down. How long could she manage without food? How long until she just slept forever? They didn't talk and just watched the girl sleeping. Could they do it? Watch her until she peacefully slipped away? And how long would it take for them? They squatted in the road and picked at some flowers that had found their way through the broken concrete. Could they eat them? It wasn't a place to make a fire, not one that couldn't be seen. But did it matter? Drawing attention? There were so many people out here, just ignoring each other. Maybe they would have to sleep here for days, huddled together in the dark and the cold. People made fires all the time. But people were attacked because of it, all the time. Showing you had food to cook was dangerous. Benazir held his sister close to him. She stirred slightly but didn't make a noise. If he were a good brother, he would make sure she was ok, but now he just felt like a child himself, and the only thing he could hope for was for her not to suffer too much. There was not much that stood between her and death.

"Mark?"

"Yes."

"What day is it?"

"Mate, I hardly know the month. Feels like this has been going on for years and it's only days. Why is it important?"

"True. Funny that, it seems much longer doesn't it? I lost track of time?"

"I think it's months or even years everywhere else in the world. We've just noticed it here too late. Didn't pay enough attention. Why is it so important what day it is?"

"What does it matter? I just want us to have enough food to get through the week and have a roof over our head. Who cares about anything else."? Benazir got up, walked a few steps and halted, listening. There was something he could hear, but he wasn't sure what it was among all the mumbling and moaning of people. He listened again. There was nothing. "Mark?"

"Can you hear this?"

"No, what?" I don't know, voices. Somewhere. It's strange. Listen, Mark. If someone approaches us and looks kind of Christian, we're both Christians ok?" Mark looked at him frowning. "Yes, and if someone attacks us who is Muslim, then we're both Muslims. Well, it's worth a try, but I'm sure a lot of people do that. These groups go by looks not by what they're being told."

"Why do you think Muslim's are always attackers? I don't want to hurt you or be a smart arse, but Muslims have blown up Big Ben."

"Well, that's the official version. We don't know for sure. But that's not what I'm getting at. Yes, let's assume you're right. Do you think Christians and Jews and all the other religious groups will just sit there and pray?"

"No, of course not."

"Good. So, if someone approaches us we cover for each other, and we are very religious. Whatever that means."

"Ok, but what… why…?"

"I think I can hear chanting. You know, religious chanting but I can't make out the words or where it comes from exactly. And maybe the government will take care of this shit and save the city and its citizens before the place blows up, after being destroyed by criminals. But they won't be here in the next few minutes. We need to find out where this noise comes from. I'm sure I can hear women's voices, and if I'm right, they might have children. Which means…?"

"They might have baby formula. I get it."

"Or maybe they are just women who are breastfeeding."

"Yak, gross." Benazir rolled his eyes. "You're such…." He laughed. It might save my baby sister. Gross?" Mark chuckled. He was being childish, but couldn't help himself. But he tried to focus on the voices Benazir had talked about, trying to blend out everything else around them. It wouldn't have been so hard except that someone had a fight with someone else and pulled a gun. The shooting noised drowned out everything else and people were running in panic. There was a fence on either side of them, and they hid behind it waiting for the shooting to stop and for them to survive. Through a few small holes, they saw people running down the road, not stopping if someone fell. They just trembled over the poor guys. "You can't trust anyone, not even people who might have been friendly. You never know what people do when they're scared." Benazir looked at Mark with dark eyes. "I can trust you, and you can trust me. That's all we need for now. And I'm sure people can't all be bad."

"Yes," Mark said, "They can. Every single one of them. We could just keep hiding for now. But what about the chanting?"

"Maybe we shouldn't look for it." Benazir's voice suddenly got an edge that kept Mark from arguing. If we were stupid enough to believe someone would look after us, it would be our damn fault, regardless of how nice they were." He paused and looked at Mark. "What if they told us lies and really…"

"Really what, Ben? Why should anybody lie to us? What for? I mean if they wanted to hurt us, they would do it straight away but a lie? I mean we have got nothing."

"We have Aisha."

"True. But you know these perverts who like little kids… well, isn't she a bit young? Goodness me, she's a baby, and you said yourself you heard women's voices."

"There are so many crazy people around."

"Yeah. But we have a better chance with women." They had had this conversation in some form or another before. What would they do if someone wanted to snatch Aisha? And Benazir had made a promise to himself. He would do anything it took to protect his sister. Physical violence or screaming so high the attacker's eardrums would burst, and they would give his sister back to him. But now they had no choice. She would die if they wouldn't find someone to help her. She would starve to death."

"We need to find out where the sound came from. I'm sure it's a group of women just hiding because they're scared." Mark's voice sounds thin and unassuming, but Benazir wanted to believe him. He wasn't ready yet to sit and just watch his sister die. A kind of numbness overcame him about his destiny, but Aisha was a different matter. His legs kept walking, and his arms kept moving automatically. He strained his ears. For one minute seems like hours, they heard nothing, and then quiet voices hit their ears. This time they both heard it. And once they've had, it was easy to find the source. The boys just moved closer to the white-painted cottage style building, following the noise, their ears strained. They walked around what looked like an ordinary black painted wooden fence. But this fence turned out to be covering a small door in the ground from unwanted viewers. Well, it was more something like a flap on the ground. A flap leading to a cellar. They had been almost standing on in when hiding from the gunshots. Benazir pressed his right ear to the ground. "I can hear the voices. So, what are we going to do next?"

"I don't know. Knock?" Mark shrugged. "Guess we just have to prepare."

"We can't stay here any longer, Mark," Benazir whispered. "Every minute we're standing here is another minute putting Aisha and us in danger. We've got to go somewhere. And this is as much of a chance as anything."' Mark looked at him. "Listen to me. You'll stand behind me but move over my shoulder so they can see you. But we will cover Aisha. And we just go from there. It's the only chance we've. What have we got to lose? If we don't do it we die anyway," he whispered. Benazir nodded, thinking about it. "Ok, you knock, and I stand behind you, just like this. He moved behind Mark. His friend nodded. "Well, I guess it can't get any worse if they let us in, better than dying out here. He crouched and knocked on the cellar door. "Hello?" No answer. But the voices had stopped. He knocked again. "Hello, please help us. It's just me and my friend. We're just boys. We don't know where to go. Please. We're just thirteen years old. We don't want to harm anybody.

Please." Nothing. Everything was just quiet. These people didn't want to draw any attention to them. They were doing the right thing.

"Thirteen," Benazir spoke quietly.

"What?"

"You've told them we were thirteen."

"And? It's the truth."

"Yes, but thirteen is a funny age… for boys."

"What? What the hell are you talking about?," Mark muttered biting his lip.

"Don't you understand? If these are women…maybe not women, maybe just girls. At thirteen you can still be small and weak but think about some of the guys in our class. They are idiots, they don't think, and they're strong. They could do some serious damage. Ronald and his friends. They're our age, and they're vicious little bastards in need of a damn good hiding. "Benazir took a deep breath and crouched down. "You need to hold her for me. We need help." He pushed his lips against the cellar door. "My little sister…she's just a baby. But we have got no food." He sighed. "Please, if you can, please help." Still, no noise. The boy turned around. "Maybe we should try to find something else." Mark just looked at him. They realised what that would mean for Aisha. Suddenly there was a scratching sound on the other side of the flap. They both stepped back in surprise. The flap opened slightly, and an old weathered hand pushed through, followed by a face marked by age and framed by short, grey hair. The woman the face belonged to asked with a deep, shaky voice: "Is there anything I can do to help?" Mark nodded trying to hide his surprise. 'Yeah, thanks. That would be nice." Benazir grimaced. He turned to Mark. "We need help, all of us. I mean my sister. We don't know what to do. She should have eaten hours ago but we have got nothing, and she has stopped crying. I don't know what that means. She just sleeps all the time."

"Give her to me," the woman said. "I can handle it." Benazir looked at Mark. "Mh… well," he answered awkwardly, "I mean I can't just give her to you. I don't know you. Even if you were a doctor. I just never met…" The woman smiled. "Don't worry, of course; you can come down with your sister and your… friend. You might need help too." Mark was sweating. His head sore with pain. He wasn't sure if it was real or imaginative, but he couldn't go anywhere else, not today and didn't care anymore what they would see if they went down the cellar. Both boys just nodded. Benazir handed over Aisha to the woman and followed her downstairs, climbing down an old wooden ladder that had seen better days, but it was stable. The further down they went the stronger a strange smell became. It almost gagged them, and Benazir tried to get his stomach under control, pitching forward and trying to hold on to the ladder, his hands pushing against the warm wood. He dropped his head to his chest and tried to breathe as little as possible through his mouth. After what seemed like an eternity they arrived in the cellar. The woman turned around, smiled and handed Aisha back to Benazir. She held out her hand. "I'm Barbara."

"Mark."

"Benazir."

"You don't' talk much, uhm. Well, anyway." Barbara shrugged. "I guess it doesn't matter. We overrate talking. Destroys a lot." She smiled, almost looking embarrassed. I know it doesn't smell pleasant in here. We had a little accident with milk bottles. They broke, and it doesn't take long until they go off. You just cannot get the smell out once it's there. It's a shame because we could have made cheese. Not that any of us knows how to do it. But I guess we could have found out. What about you? Do you know how to make cheese?" She turned to Mark. "No, Ms… Mrs I… No, I don't," he stuttered. But we are more than willing to help with other things. I don't know fixing things or something like that."

"Ha-ha." Barbara laughed out loud. "Guess there will be a lot of things that need fixing in the next few weeks. Let's pray the worst will be over soon. But being honest I think the worst is yet to come. People never learn. I mean, see what got us here. Greed. People always want more and more things. They never happy with what they've got and I think we will head back to the way we were, once people feel secure again. They won't learn."

Mark too a deep breath. "I don't agree with you a hundred percent. I mean… I mean I know what you're talking about, but I don't think it's greed that got us here. Not yet, anyway. That might have happened eventually." Benazir shot him a warning look. His eyebrows furrowed but Mark continued, while Barbara just looked at him in a very assessing way. "You see. I think the problem is… I don't know what you want to call it. I mean the fact that people think they are better just because of who or what they are. You know things that just happened to them. Things that you don't work hard for. Too many people think they deserve something better than their neighbour just because they look or are different." Barbara said nothing for a few seconds and then she smiled.

"You're a clever boy, Mark. I guess there is some truth in what you said. So, do you think if we would all believe in the same thing, the world would be a better place? Anyway, it doesn't matter for now. Let me introduce you to the rest of my family, and we need to have a look at… what's the girl's name, again?"

"Aisha." Mark and Benazir answered simultaneously.

"So, she's a little Muslim just like her brother."

"I'm not sure what I am," Benazir whispered.

"He is agnostic", Mark said. "And he went to church with my dad and I every Sunday for the last few months. Long before all this happened."

"It's lovely how you lie for your friend. He must be exceptional. But don't worry. We haven't got a problem with anyone, especially when they are as young as this one here. We're all still learning. And the Lord doesn't care what we call ourselves."

The Lord? Mark mouthed the word looking at Benazir. But his friend just shrugged. Beggars couldn't be choosers. And they didn't have a choice.

"Don't worry about your sister. She looks alright. My daughter just had a little boy, and she won't mind feeding little Aisha."

"Perhaps life isn't as bad as we thought it will be," Benazir said to no-one in particular.

Barbara's pace quickened. "This way, please." Her shoes made a clicking noise on the tiled floor, leading them into the darkness. They held onto each other so they wouldn't fall over anything. Barbara just seemed to expect them to keep up. But it just took a few seconds, and they could see some lights after turning around a corner. The house was bigger than it had seemed at first. Well, they couldn't be sure they were still in or at least under the house. But the basement was large from what the boys could see in the semi-darkness. Barbara seemed nice enough when she smiled at them and they just hoped she didn't share this place with some maniacs. She gestured for them to move forward past her and they ended up in a normal-looking room. There were torches and candles providing a warm, inviting light. Apart from rough pine shelves stacked with tins, bags of potatoes and apples there was nothing unusual. There were five more people, but the room was big enough for all of them. They had sectioned some areas off with curtains, probably to give people some privacy. Barbara pointed at a black-haired woman in her early thirties sitting in some rocking chair, holding a baby. "That's my daughter, Victoria, well Vicky and these are Mark, Ben and his sister Aisha. I can call you Ben, right? Benazir is such a long name and in these days… you never know who hears it. Maybe calling your sister Alli would be a good idea." Benazir just nodded and tried to breathe, cuddling Aisha… well, Alli. "She's adorable," Vicky said without having been able to have a proper look. You're blessed to have such a pretty sister. Give her to me. She must be starving." Ben was reluctant, but there was nothing else he could do. Something was wrong, but he didn't know what it was. However, he was sure these women wouldn't hurt Alli. "Do you live here all the time?", the boy just asked while handing over his sister. She must have sensed right away that there would be food for her as she opened her eyes and started crying louder than Mark and Ben had heard her for hours. Ben smiled. The smile disappeared pretty quick when he realised that Vicky would not cover herself up while breastfeeding. But Aisha… Alli didn't care and started sucking happily. Ben looked around, so he didn't have to watch the woman. It was natural, but he was only thirteen years old, and it made him feel very uncomfortable. He focused on the other women in the room. They just sat there smiling, finding his reaction amusing. Barbara turned to him. "Yes, well most of the time we are just down here. We were hoping to sit this out, hoping that the Lord would guide and protect us. And so far he did. But we're not sure how long this will take. We have enough food, but they stopped the water and us all being here together, needing the toilet and all these things, well I'm not sure how much longer we can stay." She banged a fist against a shelf. "It's the American president. He thought it was normal and acceptable to use racist language and obscenities. I watched him on TV long before he became president and he was always using the N-word, saying the c-word, calling people retards. The Lord doesn't like us using words like that."

"But it wasn't his followers who blew up Big Ben and the Eiffel Tower and killed people in Germany. Thousands of people got killed. There were lots of events like this long before. I'm just thirteen. I know little about politics and being honest until now I was never interested. My dad was, and that's why I know about what was going on. He was constantly talking about it. He wasn't happy about the American president or the Brexit, but he didn't think they guy was evil either. My dad just thought he wasn't very educated, and that's why he appealed to a lot of people. But apparently, he's not stupid. He just can't do fancy speeches. It's not his fault that there are desperate people on the streets whose faces look blank like they're on autopilot. He's not a great president, but he's not responsible for all the evil in the world either." Barbara looked up and smiled: "Mark, we can all hear what you're saying, and I won't blame your naivety on your age. Many people much older than you think or thought the same way. The president is not responsible for the entire world's mess. As you just pointed out things turned bad long before he was president. But what he did do, and that's why he became president in the first place is, that he blamed non-whites for all the misery that had happened and made some people think they're better than anyone else. He made it look ok to be racist and sexist, to swear and be intolerant. And things like that spread like a wildfire. This makes people who don't fit into this group feel angry, and after a while when they realise it doesn't matter how good they are, they will always be blamed, they become bad. Terrible. And then you have a big explosion just like the one we just had. One group kills and the other one seeks revenge. So now, hate has spread over the globe. I doubt that was his intention, but that's what it's now. And don't forget he started to use atomic bombs. Half of Asia's in ashes." What she said made sense, if people were fooling about with other people's desperation, stirring them on, pointing fingers this couldn't end in a happily ever after. Sometimes you had to swallow what you thought so you wouldn't hurt people's egos. He remembered how historians might describe the way people had destroyed their world and maybe how this led to something much better, but perhaps everything would turn so wrong there would be no historians. Probably there would be no people. He took a deep breath. The air was still filled with the smell of sour milk, but he had become used to it now. It didn't make him gag any longer. Benazir just looked at him. There was no way to tell what his mate was thinking.

"Wait a minute", suddenly Ben stepped forward. "I hear what you're all saying, the hate that spreads and people blaming each other. I'm not sure what's the cause… if it's religion or just people's stupidity and all this would have happened, anyway. But we are where we are. We can't change what happened. So, what are we going to do? We can't just sit here and wait to die." Barbara smiled. "You're a very emotional boy, but that's not a bad thing. I think the Lord sent you here for a good reason and maybe he wants us to stay here together, die and go the heaven."

"Die?" Ben was now screaming at her. "You want to die? Are you stupid? It would be such a waste. If there is a god, he wouldn't want that." Barbara still had that strange smile on her face. "Ben, I don't want to die. I just think maybe that's what the Lord wants us to do. Relax ok. We're safe for now. This is not a suicide mission here."

"But…" Mark had spoken up. "Isn't suicide a sin and isn't just waiting for death the same as suicide. I mean not fighting for your life?"

"What makes you think we believe in sin?" Vicky asked bleakly.

Ross-on-Wye, Herefordshire
2026

In the pale silver light, the man's face looked like he was dead already. "Daddy, what are you going to do with the man? Is he going to hurt us?"

"No, pumpkin. He will not hurt us. I think he's just in so much pain that he lashed out at everyone who wanted to touch him."

"I didn't want to touch him."

"I know, pumpkin. I know. But we can't leave him here."

"Are we going to take him home? He looks weak. I think he will die soon." The man looked at his daughter. She surprised him all the time. One minute she behaved just like the little girl she was and the next minute everything changed because she showed him how her sad life had affected her. "Come here, darling." She sauntered into his arms and buried her head in his chest. "Are you scared?"

I am", she whispered. He put his arms around her thin body. "You remember when I told you I wanted to be a doctor when I was a boy?"

"Yes. I don't think you can make the man better."

"Well, I think I can't heal him. But I think we can make him feel comfortable until he dies."

"So, he doesn't have to die alone?"

"That's right."

"But he will still be in pain?"

"Yes. But not as much pain as he's in now."

"Ok."

"Ok, what?"

"We can take him home. He won't hurt us."

"Ok. You know you're such a good girl. Even after all you've been… Never mind."

"He's big. How are we going to move him?"

"I'm not sure. I guess, we have to wait until he's better, until he wakes up and maybe he can walk. We'll work something out to help him. "He just looked at her. Deep inside him, he wanted to help the man. He didn't just want him to die here. But he was dangerous. He didn't seem to be aggressive, just desperate. Maybe he just tried to cling on to something because he was dying. The little girl's father though that at his age he should be well past the terrors of his childhood, but memories crept up on him, like tongues licking his emotions making him wonder if he was making a mistake by looking after this guy. He had dealt with fanatics before, and it hadn't ended well. The memories grew more transparent and more precise in his mind. These things were long gone, but he still remembered every detail. He didn't want to think of it, but he couldn't help it, and now his heart beat so hard and fast that it felt like falling right out of his chest.

"We need to do the best we can." The little girl said.

"What."

"We have to try our best. Isn't that what you always said. You have to help people because you're a doctor."

"I'm not a doctor, pumpkin."

"I know you didn't go to a doctor's school but you know things, and you want to help sick people to become better. That's what doctors do." Her world seemed to be so simple sometimes, and maybe it was. "I guess we can build something to carry him. We can take these two big branches over there. I can use his jacket to wrap it around like this," He had taken the man's jacket off and tightened it around to big wooden sticks. "He can rest his head on it, and I do the same with my coat. See, just like that. I think it won't last long. They will probably break apart, but maybe it will last long enough to get him to the house." The girl smiled, but she said nothing. The man would die, but they had enough human emotions left in them to care and not just leave him there. Dangerous or not. The girl's father thought the man would probably not survive until morning, but he didn't tell her that. He felt sorry for her, even though she didn't seem frightened or upset by what had happened. She hadn't cried when she was being attacked. She had seen so much already. And everything had happened so quick, but even now she didn't think of herself and her safety. They walked back through the dense forest pulling their self-made stretcher. Last night's rain had wet the ground which made it more difficult to pull it, but the girl's father moved it for longer than he had thought he could until the jackets finally ripped. The man moaned, and the girl gripped his hand. "We're almost home," she whispered. You can sleep in my bed for a while. Daddy made it. Even though it might be too small for you." The man opened his eyes and smiled at her. The girl's father bent down, twisted his body and put the man's right arm over his shoulder. He pulled him while standing up at the same time. He almost buckled. Even though the man was not heavy for his height, he was still a grown man, but the girl's father carried him on his back the last few metres to their house. The girl opened the creaky wooden door for them, and he just put the man on the ground, panting heavy. "This is where I sleep. My bed is the one standing against the wall." The girl pointed straight ahead into the almost circular looking room with its walls covered by dried mud. Her *bed* was a simple collection of criss-crossed twigs and tree branches covered by dried leaves but it looked comfortable. The man craned his head to look up. His eyes rolled in his head. He was getting dizzy. But he liked what he saw. The *house* wasn't perfect but it wouldn't collapse over their heads. Some strong pillars held up the ceiling, but this was just an extra safety measure. The rounded ceiling could hold itself. "How the hell did you know how to build this?" he mumbled. The girl's father just smiled. "I read a lot when I was younger."

"Will he sleep in my bed then?"

"Pumpkin, I think he needs to sleep in my bed. He's a tall guy. Otherwise, his feet will tangle in the air." The girl giggled. Cold daylight fell through the door still standing open. They didn't care.

"I think I can walk to the bed," the man whispered. "If you just support me." The last few steps seemed to take forever, but finally, the man sank on the bed, moaning with pain and a sense of relieve. "I don't understand how you came this far with your illness. It's at a late stage."

"You mean, cancer? You can say the word. I don't mind. It will change nothing for the better or the worse." He sighed. "It's strange, do you know that I've never been a very religious man? That's just changed recently. I guess it's just out of desperation. Does the Lord love desperate people? I don't know."

"But you scared my little girl. I'm sure the Lord, if he exists, would not like people who scare little children."

"I'm terrified."

"I know. But that's not my daughter's fault. And despite your behaviour, she wanted you to come home with us because she doesn't want you to die on your own."

"Do you think I shouldn't have come?"

"No, look that's not what I'm saying at all. We're all stressed out with what's going on over the last few years. It left marks on all of us. And I'm not sure what will happen. If there is a future for any of us."

"Well, there's no future for me." The girl's father didn't reply. The man just looked at him and smiled. "You know I've realised I haven't even introduced myself. I was occupied," he smirked. I'm Cliff."

The man shook his hand and told the man his name.

Later in the night, the man woke up in the darkness because he heard a scratching noise. He lay with his eyes wide open with his hands trembling. Something was happening. Was it the Lord? Was he finally here?

"Dad?" He could hear the girl's voice trembling. "Daddy?"

"Shh. It's okay. He's asleep. Everything is fine. Go back to sleep."

"What is it?"

"Nothing, I think it's nothing."

"I'm scared."

"Don't be. There's nothing to be afraid of. Not today."

"But I can feel something."

"It's nothing. Go back to bed, or you wake your daddy."

Something was coming nearer. Cliff heard it growing louder. It wasn't his hands trembling. It was the ground. Something moved underneath them. The ground shook.

"Pumpkin, are you ok?" Of course, the movement had woken the girl's father. He got up and lit a candle. The girl ran up to him, clinging to him and burying her head against his chest.

"It's all right. Don't worry. I think it's just a little earthquake."

"I'm so scared."

"I know. It's all right. Cliff? You're ok?"

"I think so. I didn't know there are earthquakes in this area."

"They're not normal. But it's gone now."

"What was it, daddy?"

"An earthquake, we think, it's gone. We'll be right." Cliff turned to the girl's father. "I don't want to worry you but are we safe in this… house? I mean it's underground. It doesn't matter for me, but I guess you have a little more time left on this planet." The man was honest enough to admit that it might be safer to go outside, but he didn't like to have his daughter outside after dark. It wasn't as if Cliff would be much help."

"Maybe it's the Lord wanting you to go outside for a reason," Cliff smirked.

"Don't be stupid."

The man had grown to know Cliff as a person during the last few hours. Cliff had opened up after the man treated him with curcumin and his pain had become more manageable. It wouldn't last long but it was enough for now. It had given him time to think about the coming days.

"I can't help it." Cliff sighed.

"What?"

"Being stupid as you call it."

The man turned to face the door of his house, just staring.

"I'm sorry." He got up and walked towards the door hesitating to open it.

"Don't worry. I think it wasn't a strong earthquake," Cliff said.

"I'll have a look," the man whispered. Slowly he walked into the cool night, looking at the forest, smelling the faintest breath of fern and blueberries in the air. He looked around, holding his gun in front of him, pointing at nothing in particular. He realised it would be impossible for him to see danger early enough to shoot, so he let it drop. The moonlight was bright but not enough for him to see clearly. He checked the ground as much as he could and couldn't see any cracks showing they should leave. "Well," he said when he walked back in. "I think we'll be ok."

"Are there mines in this area?" Cliff asked.

"Mines?" The girl and her father asked simultaneously.

"Yes, you know coal mines or something like that."

"What's a mine?", the girl asked. Both men smiled. "Don't worry, pumpkin. I'll explain it later." He turned to Cliff. "I know what you're thinking. If there is, maybe one of these mines has collapsed. "Cliff nodded. "Only an idea. I'm not an expert. Ow." He put his arm around his stomach.

"Are you ok?" the girl asked. "Not really. I'm sick. But it's ok. Don't worry. Only a little pain. Do you have more of that stuff you gave me earlier? He turned to the girl's father. "I think it would be a nice time of night to walk? It seems so peaceful. But I'm in too much pain. But boy would I like to smell the forest, looking at it, maybe even staying up all night, just walking until the sun rises. I haven't seen a sunrise for such a long time. I've always been hiding." They all just sat there in silence and finally the girl said, thoughtfully, "You know, I'm not afraid of you anymore." Cliff looked at her surprised. "Why should you be?"

"Because you jumped at me. But you're a nice man… And I understand. You thought I could help you. I want to become a doctor like my dad.

The girl's father looked at them. "I think I still have some painkillers. Wait, a second." He climbed on a small tree trunk and got the herb down from a shelf. When he turned around the girl was sitting next to Cliff. He remembered his father sitting on a female patient's bed like that once when he had been a little boy. He remembered the fear in the woman's eyes and knowing that she was dying. He took a deep breath and tried to concentrate on the here and now. Even though it was a mixed memory when it came to his feelings. He walked towards the two people and handed the medicine to Cliff. His daughter had his arms around him, inspecting him for injuries. Of course, it was all pretence. She didn't know what she was looking for. She'd just watched her dad many times, and he'd had his knowledge from books. Her father sat down and watched Cliff drink. After a couple of minutes, it seemed to work. The man's face turned soft with relief. "It's strange, isn't it?"

"What's strange?" the man asked. "How we've all changed. I mean, when you were a boy would your father have taken in someone who just attacked you. It seems strange. But then I guess… maybe that's the famous mysterious ways. The girl's father laughed. Somehow Cliff amused him, and he could understand why he couldn't let go of his belief. "Well, I think if I would be in your… situation, maybe I would be a believer as well. But what interests me more than anything, what do you believe. I mean you say the Lord. And I heard this word so many times but what does it mean?"

"The evidence is rock solid," Cliff said. "He appeared to me. I saw him."

"You saw the Lord?" the girl asked excitedly.

"She, pumpkin. Wait. He might…"

"Yes, I saw him. Once. I was desperate. You know when the sores started.

I knew what it was. I had seen it with so many other people."

"How does he look like?" the girl shouted. Both men burst out laughing.

"I just can't believe you saw him. Dad's certain he doesn't exist."

"And what do you think?" Cliff's eyes focused intensely on the little girl's face.

"I think it's someone we used to know. I heard that name before. But I don't know what it is. Some people told me it's a man who built the world, and he will look after us when we die, and everything will be so much better. We won't be scared anymore, and the sun will shine all the time, but we won't have to hide from each other. Because nobody wants to hurt anybody. Nobody is sick or hungry. It sounds nice." Leaning back Cliff relaxed for the first time since dawn. He was just looking at her.

"Yes, it sounds very nice," the girl's father said. Weariness flowed upwards from a place deep in his stomach. He hadn't slept well in the last few days, and the last thing he needed was for his daughter hoping for something that would never happen.

If he would let Cliff continue, he might convince his daughter. The thought let anger seep through his whole body. He wasn't sure if he could stay quiet if that happened. He wasn't fair and there were nice ones, but so far he had met none. The only reason he didn't worry about Cliff was that he was sick and too weak to do something stupid.

He had a bible. His daughter wasn't aware of it. He had put it in a little bag inside his coat, where he kept everything that he needed to protect against pickpockets. He remembered telling his daughter over and over again that she shouldn't talk to strangers. If someone tried to take her hand or made promises that sounded too good to be true, she should pull her hand away and run. If they held on too tight, she should scream and bite. But there was no protection against slow and friendly bribe.

The book had been his father's. His old man had never been a very religious man, but he had followed certain Christian traditions. It was a nice thought, but somehow things had never added up. The stories had always turned into something the man couldn't accept. He remembered the woman touching him. At night. He was exhausted and scared and had just woken up from a nightmare. A nightmare that had continued and turned out to be real. It had been a nice loving touch. Her smile had been perfect – not cocky but shy, almost as if he'd had a choice. It had looked like a smile with no intent, but it was false. And he knew it. She wouldn't accept a No. Back then, the man had known for a long time that he had been raped and it continued for too long. He had only spoken about it once and when he had finally admitted it to his friend; he had thought it might have been a mistake. The woman hadn't been the only one assuming it was ok. Apparently; it was something about god's will and having babies. All the men were dying, so the boys had to do men's jobs. Of course, it was a lot of rubbish but after being brainwashed for a while it was easy to believe it. Easier than facing his feelings of being abused. He never felt adorable even though she had told him on various occasions. At that point, he hadn't even known anymore what he was. And if being adorable meant being touched and aroused against his will, he didn't want to be adorable. But of course, being thirteen years old, he never had a choice. "I think we should go to sleep now," the man said. And the girl obeyed. They would be safe tonight. The structure of the house was sound. Cliff had smiled, but it didn't have the desired effect because he only showed his blackened teeth. They would continue the way they had for the last year. Collecting herbs and trying to prepare for the winter. Cliff would be no longer here once it started getting cold again. The dog was quiet, but he never went near the man. Almost as if he wasn't sure what to think. The girl's father agreed. For now, he didn't mind, and pain was pain. He was glad when he could make it go away. And that was all that counted. Every once in a while the girl would ask them and she would listen more to Cliff than to her dad. But that was just because she knew what her father was thinking. She wasn't stupid. That was the reason she was still alive. The man looked at her and wondered why children always wanted to be adults. What's nice about being a grown up? And what's so great about still being alive? He pushed the thought to the side and fell asleep. When he woke up, having had nightmares, as usual, it was late morning, and the girl and Cliff had already made breakfast. "She's clever," Cliff said when he saw the man was awake. I was reading through the book with her, and she almost knows everything. If she would have gone to school, she would have won a scholarship, I'm sure."

"How are you today?" the man asked.

"Still in pain, but she mixed me a nice little bit of medicine that dulls it quite a bit. Makes me woozy but the Lord spoke to me this morning. So, it's alright. It never really goes away, and it makes my mind sharper. I hear things better."

"You hear what?" the man snapped. "Voices?"

"God's voice." The man wasn't sure if Cliff with his straight face was joking or being serious. So, he told him straight he thought he was a nut. Cliff jerked to the right, staring at him intensely but then his gaze went to the little girl, and he smiled. He remained upright and started wobbling slightly. "Man, you really can take the fun out of just about anything." The girl's gaze wondered between her father and Cliff, hesitated but said nothing. For a few minutes, none of them said anything. Slowly, but deliberately, Cliff pushed himself up. He was clearly in pain but seemed to ignore it. "If you have such a problem with me being here I will leave. I thought I would be dead by now. Well, looks like I'm meant to stay a bit longer." He panted. "I don't feel great but I'm still breathing because the Lord wants me to. But if you don't want me to talk about it… I stop."

"No. I want to hear more."

Both men stopped at the sound of the girl's voice. Her father frowned. There was a grim set to his jaw. He realised there was no point of return if he wanted to keep a good relationship with her. He had tried his best to keep her away from religion, but she had to make her own decision.

"Tell me more about it," she breathed. They would fly into the dark and unknown territory. He would lose her. She would get hurt. God had held nothing nice for him. Every time there seemed to be light after a prayer it was shattered. The only one he could rely on was himself. There was no magic power, no saviour. But how could he make that clear to her? He saw that she was only a little girl searching for the lights of a better life. Hope for a future. He couldn't give her that. All he could do was to teach her how to survive. But the controls were shattered, and now it was up to her if she could accept the way things were or if she would drown in search for a miracle. *I want to be a child again*, he thought. Innocent and trusting. "Go on then. Tell her more," he said with a dead voice. "But tell her everything. Not just the good bits. Tell her about history, the bible, how people slaughtered each other and like there was meant to be a saviour but how people killed in his name, again and again, and again. And how god, your god, killed people because they didn't worship him. Your vain god."

"Look, mate," Cliff said reassuringly. "I never said I'm a Christian." He looked hard-eyed and self-confident. "I'm not blind and don't ignore what people did. But I'm not one of them. And it's not the Lord's fault if people do the wrong thing. I'm not sure about the details. I just believe in a creator, and I believe that life does not end with death. There's more after that and that after depends on if we were good people. By god I don't mean going to church, a synagogue or a mosque, praying five or a hundred times a day or hopping on one leg chanting some nonsense."

"That would be difficult for you at the moment," the little girl added. Both men looked at her, and they all burst out laughing. "You're right," Cliff chuckled.

"So, what do you believe then?" The girl and her father questioned at the same time.

"Well, you see I had a family once and when they were gone… when it was just me, I believed in nothing. It was a long journey for me. But you must believe me I'm a good man. I might have a little sick sense of humour sometimes, but I'm not that bad. If we do our best to be good people, if we are nice to each other, help each other, don't be greedy, god will welcome us with open arms. I don't think he wants us all to go to the same place to pray or follow certain rituals. Really doubt he has time to watch us all every second of the day to find out what clothes we're wearing."

"So, you don't think god will like me more if I read the bible that dad has hidden in his bag?"

"What?" The girl's father turned ash-grey. "How do you know about it?"

Cliff laughed so hard he had to hold his tummy because he was hurting so much. His face had turned as red as a ripe tomato, but he couldn't stop. His laugh subsided into a quiet giggle, but tears were now running down his face.

"Are you ok?" The little girl frowned.

"Yes, little one. I am. You've just discovered something, and you didn't realise. You see your dad keeps saying he does not… believe. But then he hides a bible. That's hilarious."

"Why, isn't the bible just a book. A historical book that tells us something about the past and not necessarily the truth. A book that you should see in the context of its time?"

"Wow, where did you get that from. Who told you? These words can't be your own. I mean you're five years old. And I can say to you… you might be right. But I'm not a Christian. Not the way people used to be growing up with the church on Sunday and the powerful impact of a Jesus looking painful. I think that was too deliberate, trying to brainwash people to follow particular churches or sects like herds of sheep, where people have to have a specific colour of skin or upbringing. I started to think about a god that could exist and realised most people were hypocrites. They all think their belief is the only true one. But they just twist it to their own needs. There's a wonderful German word for that. It's called Wendehals. It means someone who just goes with the flow, has no real opinion of its own and only says what people want to hear. I guess there's a Wendehals in all of us to survive. But you see, little girl if you're going to have a future you have to have an opinion about things, how you want them to be and why. That's of great importance, the why. Following someone and not knowing why, always backfires. The girl's father nodded. He knew an abundance about trying to escape and not following his gut feeling. First, he had faith in the saviour from the government, and when that didn't happen, he had tried his luck with religious people. As a boy, he trusted Christians must be good people. That's what they had taught him in Sunday school. But there was so little tolerance, and in the end, it was these people who had hurt him the most. But it didn't matter. Most of them would presumably be dead, and he was a man now. The girl knew nothing about it. She had been far too young to remember. She barely remembered her brother who had died trying to protect her.

London September 2020
Mark and Benazir

"I'm sorry… I just assumed. Perhaps it made sense for me. Well, I grew up as a Christian and you talking about the Lord, well that's typical Christian speech. Sorry, I didn't want to cause any problems. I'm tired of arguing." Mark just sighed. Benazir just wanted to get out but wasn't ready to admit it. These people just seemed so strange, but they offered them a roof over their head, food and baby formula for Alli. It would be suicide to leave today. Barbara just smiled, and their talk turned to other matters. "Justice", someone said.

"What?" Ben and Mark spoke at the same time. Barbara stood up again. "We just want justice. And we know there is a higher power who will give us that." Ben rubbed his eyes. "What else is new?" Barbara was irritated, but she recovered quick. "Well, we all believe in the same god, right? You're a Muslim, and you believe in that god." It wasn't a question but a statement. "To be honest, I have no idea what to believe at this point. All I'm worried about is Ally's safety, and I'd love a coke. But I will not get that, so I'd just love to know Alli is safe."

"That's very noble of you but what about you. Aren't you worried about yourself?" Barbara smiled, but it looked false. "Well, of course, I want to live, and I'm tired, and I'd love to have time for myself, but that's just wishful thinking. Everybody with power is gone. I don't know where they are but they aren't doing their job, and we're not going to get a normal life anytime soon. Thanks to the American president and his allies in Europe who had nothing better to do than push the racism to a level they couldn't control, to a point where people are just at each other's throats." He slumped down on the floor and leaned his head against the wall behind him. "I don't want to think about what I want right now, worrying about Alli keeps me sane. And I need to find a place where she can grow up relatively safe. This is fine for tonight, but I don't think we can all stay here forever.

"It's late, Ben," a voice yawned. It was Vicky. "I think we should go to sleep now," she whispered. People just nodded and answered with noises that sounded like agreement. They just laid down where they were and just snuggled close to each other. Nobody seemed to have a wash or sleep in another room. "Night, Mark, night Ben."

"G'night, all of you."

A warm front came in about midnight. Mark could feel it. He was wide awake and just stared at the ceiling. After a while, his eyes had adjusted to the darkness, and he started to make out shapes. He observed the sanctity of the room he and the others were laying in, listening to their quiet breaths. He began to feel sloppy contemplating about how long he'd had no shower. He touched his hair realising how oily it felt and began to wonder how long these women hadn't washed. They didn't seem to stink, but maybe the smell of soured milk had covered it. He wasn't in the least bit sorry that he had left home. They didn't have a choice, but he still thought they weren't very well prepared for what was to come. His mind wandered. "It is not becoming a young boy to flirt with grown women," a voice whispered.

"What?" Mark's head jerked to the right. He gave a wry laugh. "What?" he asked again.

"Be quiet, sweetheart. Mark." A female voice whispered. "Mark." She repeated his name softly then a dry hand touched his arm, stroking it lightly. He was more aware now that he hadn't washed. "You're responsible," the woman scolded, "for keeping quiet, for not waking anybody. Understand it?" "Yes mam," Mark said automatically.

"If anyone… if anyone wakes up someone might hear us. You know, someone from the outside. These men might come in. These bad Muslims or the lying Christians."

"What are lying Christians?" He noticed how the woman's hand was still stroking his arm slowly moving towards his hand. He tensed. "These are the men who say they are Christians, but they don't live the way Jesus told us. They're liars. They will burn in hell. We have to stop them. Can't you see? That's why he sent you here. There aren't enough of us. Nowhere near enough. We have to make more. Don't you agree?"

"Agree with what?" She didn't answer. "Are you uncomfortable, Mark?" she just asked. He was longing for sleep. He'd been awake all day, but he didn't want to close his eyes. Not now. "Well?" she asked again softly, her fingers moving through his hair. Mark guarded himself. "I'm not sure what you are saying." He couldn't see it, but he could hear her smile when she answered. He whispered back wearily: "I don't understand." She let his words trail. All he wanted was to go back to sleep. But she moved even closer. The stroking continued. It had wandered down his arm to his armpits, now stroking the side of his ribcage. Mark noticed a strange sensation between his legs. It was familiar, but somehow it was different this time. He had never felt ashamed of being aroused before. It just used to be something that occasionally happened in the morning, when he rose early, barely remembering what he had dreamed the night before. The woman whispered to him, but he couldn't concentrate on what she was saying. All he could feel was her touch making him feel ashamed and stiff at the same time. He moved with a start, and her hand jerked away. All these women in the room with them and she was coming after him. Why? How could she? He rubbed his eyes. A dream? No, more a nightmare. The wet dreams he usually had differed from what he was experiencing now. He heard her laughing. "Don't be shy. These feelings are normal. But this is what the Lord wants. Trust me." She had not covered her front bits. He could see her white breasts and realised it was Barbara. His eyes had adjusted to the dark. Mark wished they hadn't. Her body was bony. It reminded him of his aunt, even though he had never seen her naked, but she was just as skinny. Mark needed to get away from the woman but he couldn't. His froze just looking at her. There was a turning or moving. Only her hand. It continued as if nothing happened. There was just one choice now. He had to push it away. He didn't want her to know he had a hard-on. It felt wrong. It was too intimate. To his right loomed the dark grey of a room with no artificial or natural lights. He could hear some people snoring lightly, but maybe they were just pretending. He still felt embarrassed, but it was more than that. It was a strange fear rising in his middle bringing up all the sour bile from his stomach.

"D'you like this?", she asked.

"What?" He couldn't believe she just said that. He had come here to feel safe. He had thought they were nice people who he and Benazir could become friends with. People that would fight with them and maybe most of them were. Well, the fighting part. But he just realised what she had said. She wanted to extend this… group… or whatever it was. But not by adding a stranger to it. This was some weird sect with a serious issue. They had no problem having sex with children or teenagers, which wasn't much better. Goodness, he wasn't even sure if he could father a child. He was only thirteen years old. "Is this what you do all day?" He heard himself whisper. Her hand stopped. "What d'you mean?"

"Pray to god to send you a boy to have sex with." There was silence. Her hand had not started moving again. Maybe that was it. Maybe he just had to force her to look in a mirror. His body was shaking, and she noticed it. She smiled again. He could see her teeth glowing in the dark. It wasn't difficult for her to realise he didn't feel as confident as he pretended to be. He wanted to get up and run, but his body still didn't want to follow the command. He felt like his feet would move like running in the deep snow with lead weights on his feet. The resistance would quickly wear him down, and she would catch up. He wouldn't be able to get away. Mark glanced back to the way they had come in, but he couldn't see much. And finally, he just gave in to whatever she was doing to him. Even when she climbed on top of him, started moving and he felt like throwing up he did nothing. Nothing. Not even a "no" left his mouth. She wouldn't have cared, anyway.

When he woke up the next morning, she had gone back to her place. Everybody behaved normal as if nothing had happened. People told him, that Mark and Ben could stay as long as they liked. Their stock was still high, and maybe they could sit the whole thing out. Mark just shrugged. He didn't care. All he wanted was a shower. Let the water wash away all the dirt. Stand there for hours. There was no shower. But these women had to wash somewhere. He recognised that. They didn't smell too bad unless his sense of smell had changed entirely in the last few days. And Ben? Well, he was happy with it all. It didn't seem like someone had touched him. Maybe because he looked like a typical Muslim. Whatever that meant. His friend was watching these women taking care of Aisha. He could be thirteen again and just be a boy for a while. Could Mark destroy this by telling him they would leave? Maybe last night had only been one night. Something like an initiation. Maybe they did this to all newcomers. Something like a weird test, if they deserved to stay there. To check if they could keep their mouths shut. And, he still had the gun. He imagined pushing the barrels against the woman's skull and how it would muffle the sound of a shot. But she was capable of killing him. And she had the support of the group. She may look innocent and sweet, but she wasn't. He learned that last night. He was about to tell Benazir what he had been up to, what these women were capable off, but he felt a strange sort of shame. What if he was the only one? What if Ben hadn't been abused? His friend looked pretty happy. Would he let these people take care of Aisha if they had done the same to him? Mark just sat still, listening, watching, trying to figure out what his next step should be. There was a faint continuous murmur of voices coming from people going about their routine daily tasks. The air in the cellar felt suddenly too warm. There were no windows. All he wanted was to get out. This place had felt so unique. Almost like a sanctuary just for a moment. But this had changed in only one night. It was too bad they couldn't stay here and wait until the world had returned to normal. Only then Barbara came up from behind him and wrapped her arms around his waist. "What are you doing here? We need your help over there."

"What again?", he almost screamed. She just giggled and grabbed his left hand, still laughing. "We just need you to lift something. Only over there. We're going to cook potato soup tonight, and the sacks are a bit heavy. I mean you're a man. You can do this.

"I'm not a man. I'm thirteen."

"You're a man, trust me. I felt it last night."

Mark just felt sick and pulled away his hand. "I can't be… believe you have so much food here. This place is… is gr… great"

"Much better with you here", she whispered. Mark sighed.

"It's too bad."

"What?" "That we have to leave soon."

"Why?" Her voice was dark, filled with something like anger. "You know why. It's far too risky to stay in one place for too long. Especially with Aisha. And you have a lot of people here. You will run out of food, eventually." She looked him in the eyes, looking like she was trying to read his mind, smiled and then blurted out. "Stay." People stopped what they were doing and started to look at them. Mark searched her eyes for the truth. Why did she want him to stay? Did she care or did she just want to continue what she had done last night? Was she scared he would tell someone? Or did her friends know, anyway? Would she be lying to him? In as calm a voice as he could muster he asked, "Why? Give me one good reason, why."

"Well… Ben, wouldn't want to leave. I don't think. His sister's safe here."

"But we cannot stay here forever." Mark's hands were shaking.

"Life's complicated, you see. And we just have to trust the Lord. He will work something out. You know I'm right." She touched his arm lightly, and he winced. "I'm not sure about the Lord, but I don't want… this", he whispered, but she hadn't heard him. She was just walking off to talk to Barbara. Mark couldn't shake off the sense of being sick, but he also felt rage rising in his chest. He might be just thirteen but the last few days had strengthened him. He wasn't a child anymore. And he wouldn't just lay there every night and worry if she would try to share his bed hoping to fall pregnant. It was sick. Mark decided if that were the way she wanted to play he would not take part in it. It was working. He stayed angry. He was balling his hands into fists and spat on the floor. She didn't even notice as she had her back to him already, but her ignorance angered him, and he lost the rest of his control. He glared at her for a few seconds, then shouted, "Is that all you have to say." Dead silence. Everybody stared at him now, even Benazir. "Mark?" That's all it took. Mark was thirteen again. His courage scared him. He couldn't bear to stay another night. But he didn't want to leave either and maybe face being killed by some angry kids. He chuckled, pretending. "Sorry, I think that was louder than I intended. I just wanted to help with the potato sacks."

If she wanted to touch him again tonight, he would just let her. He would just be immobilised, again. "Mark, are you alright?" Ben repeated. He was very close now and just whispered, making sure nobody else heard. The women just smiled and continued with whatever they were doing. "What's wrong?"

"Nothing", Mark tried to smile.

"I know something's wrong. Tell me."

"Do you have any moral values?"

"I heard that expression once from my mum? What d'you mean?"

"I mean, are there certain things you would never do?"

"I… I… well… hoped I would kill nobody, but that has changed, so I guess no, not if I'm pushed enough. Especially concerning Aisha."

"That's not what I mean." Ben just looked at him, having no idea what Mark was on about.

"I mean…" Mark bent his head close making a hundred percent sure no-one would hear. I mean… you know… sex. Is there anything you wouldn't…"?

"Sex?"

"Sh… not so loud. Yes, sex."

"I'm thirteen, Mark. I haven't… well; we have to wait until we're married, anyway."

"Oh… ok. But have you thought about it? I know, we're thirteen but have you?"

"Why are you asking… Well. Okay. I guess I know what you mean. But why are you asking me to understand?" Mark's friend mouth moved into a big grin. "Are you in love? Maybe with one of these women. I mean they are so… so… old. Not old, old. But you know… old." He took a roll he had been holding in his hand, pulled it apart and began to eat it, shoving it in one chunk after another, swallowing hard, smiling at the same time. Mark still hadn't answered after he finished. Ben eyed him anxiously. "Tell me," he said.

"D'you think I can have one?"

"What?"

"A roll. I'm hungry."

"Bullshit. You're trying to change the subject. Who is it?"

"I just don't want to stay here," Mark said by way of explanation. "I just don't like it here."

"You just don't… like it here?" Ben sighed. "I don't love it exactly, but we're alive. Aisha is alive, and she'll stay that way if we stay." Mark's shoulders slumped, and he sat on the edge of a vegetable box. His hands felt damp.

"What are you saying exactly?" Ben asked. "Why do you want to leave? I mean… I mean, I know we cannot stay here forever." He folded his arms. "But why do we have to leave now? Of course, we cannot stay in this cellar for months. But I'm sure these guys have something worked out. You know, how to get supplies and so on. To stay alive." He turned and reached behind him, taking an apple out of a wooden pallet. "They have food. Real food. And they have baby formula for Aisha. There are no babies here. Aisha can live on this stuff for years." Unconsciously, Mark fastened the buttons on his shirt, even though he was wearing a t-shirt underneath and it was warm in the cellar. Almost as if he was protecting himself from a gust of freezing air. "I told you I don't like it here. These women creep me out. I mean, don't you find it strange that there is no man here. So many women and no man. Don't you find that strange? Oh yes, and no kids either. It gives me the creeps." Mark shivered. From the outside, they could hear a burst of machine-gun fire and screams. Benazir just looked at him. The noise hadn't been very loud. The sounds were absorbed inside the cellar. It almost felt unreal. But they had heard it.

"You heard it as well, right? I mean, d'you want to go out there now? Ok, these women might be a bit creepy. But do I wonder why there is no man? No, I think their husbands and fathers have been killed or are fighting somewhere, and they just got together to protect themselves. Yes, ok they are a bit religious, and we've seen what this can turn into. But they are women, how violent can they get, considering they're not hungry and don't have to protect their children. And we're both thirteen; they see us as children as well."

"No, they don't," Mark mumbled.

"Pardon?" Ben looked at him questionably. He hadn't understood what his friend was whispering.

"Nothing, maybe you're right. Maybe we're safer here than outside. Well, Aisha is." Mark just looked at his friend. He couldn't tell him the truth. There was nowhere to go right now. He turned around to Barbara. She was looking at him, smiling. It was warm in the cellar, sunlight slanted through the little gaps in the lap leading down the ladder. Mark could see half a dozen bright red apples. They looked delicious, but Marks' stomach had turned into a tight little ball. He wanted to pretend everything was ok for the sake of Ben and his sister but he couldn't. It was still morning, but he already dreaded the night. He returned the smile. What else could he do? Barbara walked through a curtain into a part he couldn't see and disappeared from his view. Some of the women were painting the cellar walls. The smell made him nauseous. What could it be that Barbara was doing behind that curtain? He noticed some leaks. Eater was running down the patched walls, making the fresh paint efforts almost a waste of time. Barbara was still behind the curtain. He needed to find out what she was doing. What was she planning? Was she expecting anything, anybody? He couldn't stand here, just wait and let his imagination run wild. If he could catch her doing something wrong, maybe he could stop her from touching him at night. Only until he and Ben could move away again. He needed to get this taken care of right away if he wanted to catch her out. Maybe it was a waste of time. But these women seemed to do everything together, and none of them hid for a more extended period unless they needed to go to the bathroom. And that was not behind the curtain. He got up and followed her.

"Oh, Lord." Mark could hear her pray when he moved near the curtain. He stopped briefly and looked back. Nobody was watching him. They were all just going about their usual community business. Or at least he assumed it was business as usual. He turned around and realised life was never what one expected. It was usually surprising or at least inconvenient. Barbara was kneeling on the floor in what he could only describe as a storage room. Burning candles covered the ground and the bare shelves on the walls. She was facing down and away from him. He stared at her back. She didn't realise he had followed her.

"I'm sorry. I'm weak. But I did what you wanted me to do. I know he's young, but maybe he will give us what you want us to have so we can continue." He could hear the concern in her voice. It sounded like she was crying. Only now did he see the huge picture of a bleeding Jesus she was praying to. "With your will, we will be okay. I know we will. He's a man. He will give me a child. Our community will grow, and we can serve you forever. Oh, Lord. Tonight, is another night, and if he has not blossomed yet, we can wait."

What the hell was she saying? Did they want to keep him here? If he were too young to father a child, they would… wait? Wait how long? She couldn't be serious. He turned around wanting to leave her alone. He needed to make plans, how to get away from here.

"Mark?" She had heard him.

"Yes?"

"Come back here. I'm sorry I didn't explain this to you. The Lord is inviting you as well. Do you understand me?" He didn't answer, just stared at her. What did she want?

"Never mind." She shrugged. I'm just concerned about you. "I know this all looks strange to you. But can't you see? The Lord is everywhere. That's why this happened. He brought you to us. He wants us to start again. To build a new community."

"That sounds nice." Mark's sarcasm escaped her ears.

"It does, doesn't it?" She smiled a broad, toothy smile, still kneeling on the floor.

"I think these guys need my help. They seemed to struggle a bit with painting these walls, I think."

"Forget the walls. They will never come right. We need to talk about this."

"That's wonderful. I mean the Lord and all this, but…"

Barbara put up her hand to silence him.

"You have no choice, Mark. If you don't let the Lord in, if you don't follow his will, you will die."

"It doesn't seem right, and it doesn't make me feel right." He just whispered. All he had to do was keep up the pretence, and he'd soon be able to get out of there. But it was so hard when she was speaking crazy like this. He wasn't sure about the existence of a god, but if there was one, he wouldn't want an older woman to rape a young boy.

"Mark, listen. It might not seem right now, but it will. I promise." Her voice was steady. "Darling. I'm sorry, but we all have to make some sacrifices for the greater good. For our future, all our future."

"I can't believe it. How do you know what the Lord wants? That this is what he wants you to do?"

"It's easy." She held out her hand. He didn't take it. He just held on to the curtains. "What's easy?"

She smiled. "It's easy to understand. He talked to me. I mean, he talks to me every day, and he tells me what he wants us to do. What each one of my girls needs to do. What your role is. What Ben's role is. Allie's."

When she looked at him that way, she seemed to believe what she was saying. If last night would never have happened, she could almost be likeable. Mark tucked both his hands under his arms and prepared to leave. But something else caught his attention. "What did the Lord say to you?"

"Well, you cannot leave until you fulfilled what he sent you here for. I'm sure you understand."

Mark shivered. "Ok. I'm not sure Ben will understand."

"He doesn't have to. He can leave at any time. He's a Muslim. We don't need these people here."

"You can't let him go," Mark whispered. "Aisha... Allie, she won't survive on the streets. And... and, he will not leave without me, anyway." He looked at the picture of Jesus. He felt like it was almost mocking him, but he realised he had to play her game in ways he had never imagined he could.

"Allie is the future." Barbara continued. "She's just a baby. She might have been born into a Muslim family, but she's too young to remember. We will take care of her, and she will continue our legacy when we cannot continue the Lord's work."

Mark took a deep shivering breath, wiping his sweating palms on his dirty jeans. "I know. She can grow up being a good Christian. But so, can Ben. He doesn't believe in Islam. I'm sure you could teach him about Jesus." Marks' voice shook. He just hoped she couldn't hear it and realise, he was lying."

Even if it was not a direct lie. He wasn't sure what Ben had faith in, but his nervousness could be a dead giveaway that something was up."

"You're right about that and about me being able to teach him, me getting involved. But you see, the Lord doesn't want that. You know, these people are different. They... they believe so... so strongly." She sighed. "The wrong thing. They moved away from our father. Their belief is... is twisted." Her face changed as if she had tasted too much apple vinegar.

"I don't want to make the situation any more difficult for you, but I know Ben would be open to the, well, right believe. He's mentioned Jesus a couple of times and how interesting he finds him," Mark lied. "It's just awkward for him because he didn't grow up with the bible. What can I do to help?"

"I'm sorry. I'm so sorry. I know how much you love your friend but you see, we could never trust a Muslim. They're just too different. You cannot trust them. We could never know for sure if Ben just pretends or if he trusts our great Lord."

"What are you going to do then? You can't just send him away. I told you, he will not leave. I know, you could just push him out. There are so many women here, and I'm sure they would support you and not us, but I'm sure he would come back even if it were just for Ai… Allie. I know it's asking a lot but—please try." Barbara cut him off. "Of course, I can. I think it's not a bad idea. We can try. Maybe he can stay. It will put your mind at ease, knowing that your friend will be here as well, right?

"Thank you." He turned around knowing she was lying. The question was what she was lying about. How would they make Ben leave? He wouldn't just leave Mark and Aisha behind. Perhaps he would leave his sister somewhere where he could be sure someone would look after her, but after two days in this cellar they couldn't be certain, and his friend would know that. He would want to spend some more time with them so these women could convince him they were good enough people. The woman looked at him and smiled when he walked back to the potato sacks. None of them saw him staring at Benazir, putting his arms around his middle because he suddenly saw himself staying here on his own having to be with Barbara for many years to come. He couldn't do that. He would die. If he had a choice, he would rather be killed like Ben was going to be. Mark remained motionless, not knowing what to do next, just watching his friend and the others from the darkness of a corner moving around, going about their business. He took a deep breath and forced himself to walk. He had to talk to Ben. His heart was bleeding when he saw him and Aisha smiling as if they had no care in the world and they probably hadn't. He slouched not being sure what should happen now. But then it occurred to him that this was not real. Ben's happiness and Aisha being safe was an illusion. If he said nothing, it still wouldn't stay the way it was now. He was ready. "Ben," he whispered when he was close enough. He turned around. Barbara was nowhere to be seen. But that didn't mean she wasn't listening. A woman was standing pretty close, but she was busy reading a little, black pocket bible. "Hello? Ben, I need to speak to you. Now. It's important."

"Why are you whispering? Is it because you still want to leave? That's crazy, and you know it. I mean do you think I don't know what's going on?"

"What? Mark just stared at him. How could he know? "How did you…?"

"Mark, I know what they all think. They know I come from a Muslim family, I mean my name, my looks… Religious people don't exactly tolerate each other at the moment. So, I made some preparations." Benazir moved slightly to the right side.

"What are you doing? Get down." Mark hissed. "Don't draw attention to us. But Ben just smiled and ignored Mark, pulling something out of his pocket. "You see. I talked to Sylvia this morning. She's very good friends with Barbara. Almost like her right hand, in case you haven't noticed."

"I have noticed," Mark replied. Ben looked at him. His face said can't you just listen to me? He waited a few seconds and then handed over a few loose pages to Mark. "What's this?"

"The bible." He smiled. "Not the real bible, I mean all of it. That would be a bit short. You see it's an interesting story or stories if you will. It lifts people and then crushes them in an instant just as religion is supposed to be. After reading it, you almost feel like crossing yourself and thanking god for his generosity in choosing you. But deep down I know it's all a lot of rubbish. But that's not what I told Sylvia. These pages provide hope, and that's what I told her when she showed them to me. You could call it a beginner's course." Ben smiled. "You see. I will be fine. I can pretend I want to find Jesus and they will let me stay. I can talk about the bible for years to anyone who will listen. One day they will ask me to be a minister." He grinned. "Only joking. But I'm sure I can convince them I'm a born-again Christian. I mean, it's not as if being Christian is tied to certain looks. I read a lot, not just the bible."

"What? Since yesterday."

Benazir laughed. "No, of course not. Being a Muslim, I mean a real Muslim, means you find out about Christianity. All these religions have the same origin. I always found the process quite rejuvenating. Things have changed, but I still know. So, when we arrived two days ago, and I realised what these people were all about, I had to make a plan. His fingers trailed along the racks behind him. "I left Sylvia a note saying Jesus brought me here to find out more about the right way and that I had this dream about them teaching me everything I needed to know. So, this morning she gave me these pages to study. Nothing unusual. It's just pages from the bible. I've seen it before. I think it was just a test to see if I learned about Jesus and the holy book. I think I convinced her. She invited me to one of their bible study sessions and considering that nobody has asked you… well, I guess nobody did, because you would have told me. Well, I guess it worked. I'm not sure for how long. But for now, it worked." Benazir sat down on a box and peered at the women doing useless work like painting wet cellar walls. Mark was too calm by nature to shout. If he disagreed he would just raise an eyebrow and stare straight ahead. That's what he was doing now. His instinct was telling him to run away. But he couldn't, not without Aisha. They had to stay when the one thing they should do—flee, as quick as possible—was the one thing guaranteed to get them killed on the streets. Benazir just got up, smiled and walked over to Sylvia to scoop Aisha from her, tucking her into his arm and taking the bottle from the woman to feed his sister. Mark just sat steady and quiet, watching him from a distance. He could see himself running over to the top of the staircase, pushing up the latch and just running, running, racing. But he did nothing. He just sat there.

Ross-on-Wye, Herefordshire
2026

The past didn't matter anymore. They couldn't waste time. Maybe there wasn't much left for them. They lived in a cruel place now. There were diseases and no doctors or even medication. They had to go back to the basics.

Learning how to deal with nature and what then? Every day would still be a struggle, even if they weren't sick. And that could change every day. Clifford had shown him what could lay ahead. The exploded power plants, chemicals leaking into the river. It was a miracle the planet had not been wiped out yet with all the things that were not controlled by skilled human beings anymore. Everything was just waiting to end in a catastrophe. If he wanted his girl to reach adulthood, he needed to create some protective community for her. Maybe something similar to the 17th century without all the modern technology but with all the knowledge they had gained since then. They needed to find like-minded people, to build a town away from violent people. He looked at sleeping Cliff. His skin was white, too white. The girl's father listened to his uneven breathing. He realised what he had to do now. He walked over, shaking his shoulder slightly, trying to wake him up, without alerting the little girl. Cliff frowned. He glanced at the man, waking up from a deep dream, trying to focus on what was happening. His eyes were still a bit out of focus. "What's the matter," he said uneasily, his voice croaked."

"I need to ask you a question."

"What d'you mean?"

"Before you came here, when you were on the run. Did you only meet people, who wanted to get to you? You know, real… violent people? I mean did you never meet nice people. I mean nice people you could have stayed with and rebuild something. Something good."

Cliff smiled, but it didn't reach his eyes. "If I had, I would have stayed with them. I wouldn't be here. "

They heard a noise. The girl's father was fumbling for his weapon. Instinctively they knew that the noise was coming from people sneaking around their house, they were attackers. But they hadn't realised there was a house under the ground. The man got up and snapped back the rounds from his gun. His finger moved to his lips, showing to Cliff to keep quiet. He looked through the spyhole in the door. He couldn't see much. But he thought it was… Wait, it couldn't be. He whispered to Clifford. "I think it's a child. But I cannot say for certain. I think it's a boy. I guess he's no older than… I'm not sure. Maybe seven." He looked at Cliff again. His face was twisted. "Cliff. Are you ok."? He was still whispering. Cliff shook his head. He had tried to get up from his bed but had failed. The man knew what he needed. "Cliff, listen to me. Don't worry what's going on outside. The shelf above your head… there are some painkillers. They're strong ones. Not herbal. I kept it there for emergencies. Take it. You can reach it with your hand. It's a small bottle labelled morphine. I guess I don't have to explain what it does. Take it sparingly. There are syringes as well. Make sure there's no air in them. It'll help you. I'll have a look. "

"Don't." Clifford sank back on his bed, reaching for the bottle. "You don't know if he's alone. You don't even know if it's a boy. You said so yourself - you can't be sure. What if there's someone else out there? I cannot look after your daughter. You know that. There are lots of people still out there, trying to survive. A goodly number of the people are twisted now; some are even professional fighters; you know like soldiers and the like. I know the majority are just civilians—often whole families. But I've seen a lot of godless people when I was out there. Where do you suppose they're all gone? I mean the violent ones. I tell you we cannot be careful enough. Not with your daughter to worry about." The man thought of the devastation he had seen in the last few years. How close he had been to losing his little pumpkin. Nothing ever seemed like a safe place. Fights, rapes, religious doctrines, savages. The first time he had felt something like peace was when he had finished their little house. But he had to think about their future. They couldn't do this on their own and when he had seen the little boy outside an idea had risen in his mind. Maybe not even an idea, maybe just a fragment. He turned to Cliff. "I know what you mean, and you might be right, but I think we have to take the risk." He stumbled towards the door, hesitating for one second and pushed it open, reaching out. "May I help you?" The little boy and Cliff looked up in confusion. Both didn't expect that much politeness. The boy just stood there, his eyes never leaving the man's face. "Mister." He gasped, stumbling forward. "Hey… be careful—" Cliff tried to warn the man. He staggered as he tried to get up but with no success. He was just too weak even with the morphine successfully passing through his body. The man didn't even turn around. He just stared at the boy who had seen better days. His clothes were in rags, and his face and hands were dirty to the point of having to be washed for hours to get the dirt off. The man offered a piece of dried food to him, and they boy's greedy side asserted itself. He just took it quickly and stuffed it into his mouth without stopping to look at the man's face. For a little while, nothing more happened. The man wasn't sure what to do next. The boy was dirty and had been on his own for a while, but he didn't seem to be sick or aggressive. Suddenly the boy tensed, turned around, threw himself forward and started to run. But the man stretched out his hand and grabbed his ripped shirt. The boy's short legs flicked out, and he fell headlong to the ground, scraping his knees when he landed on them first. "No need to hurry. I'm sure whatever is waiting can wait a little longer".

"Let me go! Let me go," shouted the boy.

"Why should I?" The boy shut his eyes, started to cry and balled his hands into fists at the same time. The man wasn't sure if he was angry or scared. He took a couple of deep breaths. "Calm down ok. You can do whatever you want. I will let you go. But maybe you want to rest first."

"The boy relaxed slightly. "Do you have any more food?"

"Yes, inside the house."

"What house?"

"My house. I build it into the ground."

"There is a house and food?"

"Yes."

"Is it enough?" The man didn't answer straight away.

"Why did you bother to come out? I mean why take the risk? You don't know me," the boy whispered. The man still didn't answer, why should he? He didn't know the answer himself. "Maybe because I'm tired of running away from everybody."

The boy looked at him. "Me too. Maybe I'm tired of being scared too. Either way, it comes to the same. I just accept what's coming. There ought to be more to life than running, right?"

"Right."

"It's not fun."

"No."

And you have a home? A real home?"

"Yes."

"And a child is living with you? Would he like to be my friend?"

"It's a girl."

"Doesn't matter. Would she like to be my friend?"

I would think so. She hasn't got many friends. She's got none if you don't count her dog."

"That counts."

"What?"

"A dog. That counts as a friend. I had one - a long time ago. He died." The boy said it just matter of fact. He looked at the man seriously. "They make perfect friends. Loyal."

"I guess you're right."

"Do you want more?" the boy asked curiously.

"More what?"

"Children."

"I struggle to look after the one I've got."

"Oh." The boy seemed disappointed. Somehow he appeared to be very curious wanting to know everything about the man he just met in the woods. He didn't seem to be scared at all, or maybe he was just too exhausted.

"I used to want more children," the man answered him, "but things changed. It was just a stupid dream when I was young. I wanted to be a doctor, heal people and live with my doctor wife in a big hospital where we would make all the sick children better. But that was a long time ago, and I have got my hands full with my little girl now."

"So, you never wanted a little boy? D'you like little girls better."

The man smiled. He realised where this was going. "Not all girls are nice. But mine is, and you seem to be a very nice little boy."

"I am, honest. And I can look after myself. I'm no trouble at all. I might still be very young, but it won't always be that way, and when I'm a bit older, I could help you build a better house."

"What a thought!" the man laughed. "I might take you up on that." He thought about it again. "I was dreaming about building an entire village."

"I would like that. D'you know. It's getting a bit nippy out here. Don't you want to invite me to your nice, warm house?" The man smiled and leaned down to the boy. It's not winter yet. Not that cold outside." The boy grinned sheepishly. "It's not that warm either, sir."

"Where are your parents?"

"They're dead. Died of cholera. Well, that's what the man told me, anyway."

"What man?"

"The man who picked up their bodies. He said he would bury them for me. I didn't believe him, but I couldn't have done it, anyway. And maybe they saved someone's life."

The man squatted and put a hand on the boy's arm. "What are you saying? What do you mean? they might have saved someone's life."

"Nothing, sir. Nothing. I was just scared and didn't ask questions. After that, I just kept walking, hiding, running and then I found the woods. The trees don't scare me, and I found berries and grass, and there is water as well. And I could catch some squirrels. It's not bad, really." The man shivered. He looked down the road leading away from the hidden house. "Is that how you survived?"

"Yes, and I'm very good at hiding. People scare me. I've seen a lot of people killing other people. And so many were sick. I won't hurt anybody." The boy shook his head from side to side. He looked up at the man. "Maybe it's not real. I mean maybe this is all a bad dream. My mum used to sing lullabies to me when I woke up from nightmares. But if this is a nightmare why haven't I woken up yet?" Tears had run down the boy's face. The man looked past him at a little stream coming from higher up. It was little more than a seep. He could see it moving slightly, knowing it would soon turn into a stream, filling the river further down. It was a long time since he had seen a child cry. Most of them just looked apathetic now. He got a tissue from his pocket and wiped the child's face. He held it up. It didn't look too bad. It didn't matter if it was dirty or not. But somehow he couldn't help it. Letting go of habits was difficult. "Follow me", he said. He opened the hidden door, and they went down into the earth. The door was painted brown on the inside. He had made the paint himself. For a moment he propped it open with a rock, but he wouldn't leave it like that for too long. It was too dangerous. The wind blew dried leaves and dirt behind it. Suddenly he could feel the boy clutch his hand. "I think we should close the door."

"Don't worry. Come on. Before it gets too dark. We have candles, but we need to save them for emergencies, and we can make a fire, but I don't like it, in case someone sees the smoke. But you don't have to stay in our house. It's okay if you want to go somewhere else."

"No, no. I'm fine. Honest. I'm used to the cold."

"It won't be cold. We're inside the ground. I was more talking about cooking."

The boy took one last look back. All he could see behind him was shadows. There was no single star to drive back the night and remind him of what he left behind. Gone were the artificial lights from his mother's stories, he couldn't remember. Lights that once had been illuminating the sky even in the darkest of nights. He hadn't expected to sleep in a house under the ground tonight, but he liked it. He wanted to be with the man. Somehow he felt safe with him, and somehow that seemed relevant. The man turned around. "I cannot promise you that you can stay forever. But for tonight, you don't have to worry to find a place to stay. No-one is looking for us. We are of no significance to anybody. And I'm a tough guy. They threw me into this mess when I was thirteen. I come from a small area in a city with only a handful people. Not much competition between religions. Still, it got blown up, and almost everybody got killed. But when all this is over, someday, I would like to go back and see what's left. And for now, we're safe here."

"Maybe people will learn from what happened and rebuild something. My parents told me how nice the world used to be at some point. It's not anymore. But maybe one day we will rebuild everything over again." And then the boy said something bizarre: "Have you ever prayed in earnest."

The man frowned. "What d'you mean?"

"Well, have you ever prayed to a god without pretending to believe he was there. Without trying to save yourself from bad religious people." His finger traced the door frame. He still hadn't fully entered the room. Cliff was watching from the bed, but the boy couldn't see him. The man looked into his eyes. "Come in. I think we shouldn't discuss this out here."

"Yes, he can come in and tell us his name," Cliff said from his bed. The boy jumped back. "That's not a girl."

"No, I'm not," Cliff smiled. "You've got perfect eyes. But don't stop talking. You just asked a fascinating question. Do you believe in Jesus?"

"They told me god could see things in the dark. You cannot hide from him."

"Do you believe that?" the man asked.

"My mum used to tell me stories in the dark. And her hands used to stroke my forehead while she was whispering to me. She made me forget things scared me. I think if there's a god he has hands like my mum." Cliff smiled again. "Well, maybe he does. God is in all of us somehow." The man sat down on a tree stump serving as a seat and gestured to the boy to do the same. "I was running away from religion, but it seems to follow me. The last time I prayed to god and trusted he would listen to me, was when I was a small boy. I'm sorry, but I cannot say anything different. I wish I could tell you I'm sure there is a god and everything will be ok one day, even if it means after we die. But I can't. I'm sorry. If there's a god, he must be ruthless. And maybe he created this planet and then left us to our own devices, maybe sometimes poking his finger in, creating a little earthquake…"

"Or a power plant explosion…", a little girl's voice said from a dark corner.

"No, I'm sure god wouldn't do that, even a bad one. He would create a natural disaster. That has more style." The boy turned to the girl's voice. The girl stepped forward and put out her hand. "Hello, do you believe god exists? What's your name?"

"My mum said one day when we die we will stand before god. Even if we believe we were not such bad human beings, he will turn on a TV screen and show us the movie of our life from birth until judgement day. We will hear every thought that was going through our minds, and we will say how we acted, what we've done and then god will decide."

"Okay, but that's not what I asked."

"Sorry, my name is Barrett."

"I think I'm a good girl."

"Of course, you are," her father said.

"I think god will let me in," she continued in her chirpy voice. "Where do you come from, Barrett?"

"From the West, I think? I can't remember much of it. My mum always said we came from the West."

"Did your dad never say anything?" The girl looked at him curiously.

"Not much. Mostly my mum, but they were thinking the same thing."

"Do you want a tea? I can make some. I have a lot of herbs and I know what they can heal, but some of them just taste nice."

"We can't make a fire," Barrett told her.

"Why not?"

"Someone might see the smoke. But I would like to rest. My knees are shaking. I don't get a lot of sleep." He thought about how he had been hiding in the bushes from men fighting this morning and how being here now seemed incredible. The morning was a lifetime ago. Now he felt safe. He thought it only right that he and the little girl and this man should be saved. They seemed nice. The sick man on the bed seemed ok, but he wasn't sure yet. He wasn't sure where he would sleep. All the bedroom space seemed taken unless they had some secret rooms somewhere. After all, he was only a guest. But he could sleep on the floor and told the girl's father. He had slept in much worse places. He didn't want anybody to give up their room. He could hear Cliff snoring. The man was feeble. Why was he here? He'd seen people dump others with much smaller problems. Maybe he was an uncle or something. "It's so beautiful here," he said. Everybody was laughing.

"What's this place called? The boy asked not understanding why they laughed."

"What do you mean by what is it called?"

"Well, you know. It's a house. And you always have to give your house a name."

"That's true," the man said. "The house I grew up in had a name and some others on my street had a number."

"What was it called," the girl asked."

"The meadow."

"That's a pretty name," Barrett said, "But we cannot use that name.

"What about under the hill?" the girl suggested.

"Or just call it home", said Cliff who had woken up again. "After all it's a home. It keeps us dry, and no dead bodies are lying around, turning to leather. I guess that and the fact that people can't see it from the outside makes it a home. Who cares if it has a name or not."?

"You must have seen many of them," Barrett said.

"Many of what?"

"Many dead bodies."

"Haven't we all?"

"I'm not sure. Only recently, I guess. My mum always took me into her arms and made me look away if we came across something horrible."

"Your mum was a nice lady, but she couldn't protect you from reality, right?"

The girl's father pulled another tree stump closer, as the boy still hadn't sat down. The boy didn't sit down. "My mum didn't want me to have nightmares, and she's done a good job. I mean I heard about bodies lying around, people fighting, skulls and bones on the streets. I heard it in stories too, people with missing limbs, illnesses or other horrible things but I never saw it until my parents died. My mum wanted me to become a better person in every way. She always told me I couldn't change others but I can change myself. Maybe we cannot change the world, but if we start with ourselves, we might influence others. My dad agreed with her." Barret swallowed hard. "I miss them very much. My dad always gave me so much attention, well to both of us. I know he loved my mum and me very much. In the last two years, well maybe not that long… I don't know, well, things got worse—he tried to teach me a lot, but there wasn't enough time. He showed how to make a fire, how to hunt and hide, what I should say so I don't upset people and who to stay away from. But it doesn't always work, so I stayed on my own."

"Yes, the world can be an ugly place if you're on your own." the girl's father said.

"But I'm not on my alone now," the boy smiled.

Thirty minutes later they were all sitting down for breakfast. There was no point in going back to bed again, and ten minutes after that the three of them were out looking for berries, herbs and small animals. The dog had stayed with them the whole time but had made no noise. He liked Barrett. It occurred to the man that it was the first time in a long time he hadn't worried about his little girl. So maybe there was hope after he would be gone. He looked at Cliff. Perhaps his future was something like that. Barrett looked at him, smiling. "What's the dog's name? It's…." The man laughed. I didn't name him. It was her. He nodded towards his daughter. "Do you know what? I just realised I don't even know your names. I've told you mine."

"My name's Shishi. But my dad calls me pumpkin sometimes. The girl said.

"Nice to meet you. What did you have in mind for today?" Barrett said. He was very skinny but soft-looking. He had washed out features, but was still a nice-looking boy despite his ripped clothes and dirty shoes. He seemed to try for a hard look, but all he could muster was confident. And that was probably an act. But Shishi liked him, and the man could see where this could lead to. A protector for his daughter. Barrett had already told them his parents had died of cholera and that he had left them a couple of days ago. First, he was looking for an aunt his mum had told him about when she was still alive, but he didn't know where to look. And it was too dangerous just to wander around even though there were less and fewer people. There was a man once who seemed friendly enough and had offered to take Barret with him to a place where it was warm, and he would get something to eat, Barrett had been tempted to go, but something was off, and one night he had just run away. He hadn't felt secure, and he didn't like to spend another night on the streets. Sometimes he still had nightmares about the things he had heard. His dad had died almost three weeks earlier. Barrett had almost come to accept that his parents were dead. He had wanted so desperately for them to come back but with everything he had gone through already, it was almost normal for people to die when they were young.

"Let's have a drink of water. Okay. There's a stream down there," Shishi's father said. "We need to fill our bottles as well." He took three bottles out of his backpack, handed one to his daughter and the other one to Barrett. "We don't have to go down there," the boy said.

"Yes, that's right. You know the area well?" the man asked curiously.

"I learn quick. I have to. My dad taught me. But we have to be careful and secure the area. You never know who else is down there. I mean not just people. It could be animals as well. But I guess Sammy would smell them before we see them." The girl laughed. "Of course, he would." She patted the dog's head. "He's so clever. Aren't you? Good boy." The dog wagged his tail, not leaving her side for one minute.". Barret watched them, smiling. It was getting warm fast. The sun was shining, and it looked like it would be a glorious day. The man looked at the boy who was picking some leaves from a bush. These are poison, he said and ripped it out of Barrett's hand. "We must look at everything very well. D'you understand? There are a lot of poisonous plants in the forest, but it provides us with a lot of goodness too. You just have to distinguish between the two."

"I do. My parents explained some of it to me. But we never lived in the woods. So, what do you want me to do? Tell me and I will do it."

"We both have to say," Shishi interrupted. "I know a lot already. Do you think he will be able to learn?" She turned around to her dad.

"Of course, he will. I mean look at the plant he just picked. It's not that poisonous. I think if we cook the leaves very well, it'll be all right."

"What are they?" Barrett asked.

"Amaranth," the girl and her father, said simultaneously.

"Why do you think nobody has eaten them?"

"Well, I guess there aren't too many people or animals here that have found them. Or at least I hope so. Sammy isn't barking, so I guess that's what it is. And there are so many plants in this forest, Barrett. Most of them aren't eaten, even if there are animals nearby." The man patted the boys head without intending so, and the Barrett leaned into the man's body. Sammy suddenly got nervous. He didn't bark but something was up, and the three people could soon see why when they came closer to the stream. A group of cows was grazing at its banks, drinking from the fresh water. They seemed so out of place, but somehow they looked like they belonged here. They were filthy but strangely peaceful as if nothing in the world could harm them. Some of the adult ones had calves, and in the whole, there was a group of about ten. The man remembered reading that cows weren't too intelligent. He wasn't sure if that was true, but so far none of these creatures seemed to notice the three intruders. As far as they could tell, they were all females and moved with the same speed, utterly indifferent to their surroundings. Their faces were kind of cute, and they fascinated the children. Shishi's father swallowed hard and forced himself to get closer. He had killed animals before, but he didn't intend to harm these. Maybe they could milk them, but… they had horns, and he had never milked a cow in his entire life. There was no emotion in their features but then, how could you see the feelings of a cow with their dumb dark eyes in their furry faces?

"The look of you is enough to scare them off," Shishi teased Barret.

"Hah," he laughed. "You haven't seen yourself in a mirror lately. You need a good scrub yourself." They both giggled until the man told them to be quiet. "We cannot touch them," he said. "They're not pets, and they're not used to human beings anymore."

"We won't hurt them," Barret answered. They know it, and we know it. Look at them. They're so peaceful, and I know how too milk a cow. I grew up on a farm."

"How can you have grown up on a farm? You're not much older than me," the girl scowled.

"Ok, not exactly grown up, but I was born on one, and I have farming in my blood. My mum was always talking about it and how she wanted to go back there one day when all this was over. She never taught me about the wild, though. What we could and couldn't eat in the forest. I had to learn it myself. But cows… I know what to do with cows."

"So, cows don't bother you. Prove it then. Milk one." The man just smiled. He was very sure they boy wouldn't put himself in danger. Barret squinted, looking from the man's face to his daughter's. "Alright then," trying to sound confident. Both of them laughed out loud, moving closer towards the group of animals. There was a weird noise, and they all jumped back, but then laughed some more when they realised it was coming from one calf who tried to get some more milk from its mother. The cows looked up and realised the group of people staring at them. But they didn't seem to be scared.

The stream had almost blended into the background with only a faint glow now. Barret had no desire to drink anymore. The cities wouldn't do well for many years to come but if they could start their own farm, life might be different. It was strange; he had always been a city boy, but he didn't miss it, he didn't feel much of anything. It was the time of day when he went out with Shishi to collect food for themselves and Cliff, but this was so much more than food. This could be future, a real future. Nothing he dreamed of when he was a little, but dreams had turned into nightmares a long time ago and who wanted nightmares to be true, anyway. He remembered taking to drink for a while, years ago, just to forget. Drink was always available, but for the first time in years, the man didn't feel like drinking. Not that he had touched a bottle in the last few years, but the desire had always been there. The desire to just escape this life in hell, his ruined years. He almost felt cleansed. He felt hope. He thought about the bible and how he had tried to make sense of it, the endless discussions with his friend about various religions and the realisation that none of them held the only truth, just bits of it. And that the human mind was incapable of figuring out what these bits were, incapable of putting them all together to one big picture. He walked next to Barret, trying to give him support no matter how this cow adventure of his would end. Barrett didn't want him to help. He wanted to prove he could do this. So, the man found a spot under a tree, sat down with his daughter and just watched the boy. "What are you going to do?" he shouted. "Coax the calf away and milk the mother?"

"That will not work."

"You got a better idea?"

"What about a full-on attack?"

"Attacking the cow?" the man smiled.

"Well, yeah. Walk up to it and leave the calf where it is. It's not sucking. So…"

The girl was now standing guard, not trusting the whole situation, wondering the while what would happen next and how Barrett would manage. But she felt no guilt for not helping. It was like watching a car accident. People just couldn't help it. Barrett asked for a rope. But they didn't have one. "Well, I'll tell you I will milk this cow and if it's the last thing I do," Barrett laughed nervously.

"I haven't had milk for ages, "the girl grinned. "Maybe we will have some tonight if that cow doesn't hit you with its horns." The man addressed his daughter. "Don't scare him."

I'm not scared," Barrett shouted. "What about you Sammy," he called out to the dog. But he was clearly unsure what to do having never seen these strange animals before. He sat by the girl's side just in case she needed protecting or maybe he was just a coward. The man put his pack and the gun next to him. The sun was up now, standing fully on the horizon. Midday. Birds were sitting in the trees, watching. Barrett was making his way through the dense grass, across the small wild field. He had to be careful but they're not wild animals. If they remembered human contact positively, he would be fine. But did they? He remembered his father once explaining how meat was produced, how they kept cows in tight spaces, pumping them full of hormones, something called mass production. But they had normal farmers as well. He just hoped this group belonged to the latter. He was convinced it was all about having a good stare, making the animals think he was in charge. The boy paused at the stream. He had to walk through it and he would make a noise. Really, he'd just like to do it, get up the small bank and get it behind him and over with. Even though he's just a small boy, life had made him grow up quick. He should slow down, approach them carefully, have a look around, so he would not get hurt. However, his boyish instinct just told him to run, keep going, finish it. He didn't want to die or get hurt. For the first time since his parents died, he cared what happened to him and he wanted to take care of the man and his daughter Shishi. She called him by his name, not a nickname or worse something like the c-word. He had heard that too often in his short life. He was a person to them. So, he forced himself to slow down because there was no other way. He wanted to stay with these people, waking up together, find food, just be safe and it was strange, but he wanted the man to be proud. The closest cow was looking at him now but she didn't move, just continued to chew. If he could get some milk, they would be fine. The years wouldn't be so long anymore and so similar. Things would change. And they would change for the better. He's embarrassed realising how much he liked the girl, she's pretty and so calm. Most kids were just scavengers, they bit and screamed and tried to hurt him, but she's different. Very different. He could see how her dad had made it possible. Like his parent's love was still with him, even now. They wanted him to be happy, even though it was hard work and things weren't easy anymore. Now, it was time for good things. And it would all start with some milk he could give to them. Anxiety dug its fingernails into Barrett. Someone else who might have seen him would think he would run in the opposite direction but he didn't. Barret shook his head, tossed a small stone aside and continued. He ran through the stream. It was only once he was down on the small field that he looked back at the man and Shishi. The boy turned around, opened his eyes wider, staring at the cow in front of him. "I do what I have to do," he mumbled to himself. He didn't quite believe it, but he would do it, regardless. Barrett stepped forward, looking at the calf which didn't seem to be interested in the slightest. He looked at the mother cow again. "I barely remember cows but I know I saw one once, and I milked it together with my grandma," he said. "And I remember I liked it. But does it matter? I guess not. If you just give me some of your milk, we leave you alone. See this little girl over there. She needs some to stay healthy." The cow just stood there, then she walked towards him with a limp, still monitoring her calf. But for some reason she wasn't scared. Maybe she still remembered humans in a good way. Maybe this small group got away early enough before humankind turned into heartless scavengers. It didn't matter. They were here now. Barrett stepped closer, bending down. He put one hand on the cow's head. She still looked at him not moving. He put all effort into ignoring her calf, so she would not feel threatened. It seemed to work. She just stood there. His hands started stroking her fur. He couldn't be sure but she seemed to like it. Her brown eyes focused on his. "What do you think will happen to us, to all the people that are still alive?" Barrett asked. The cow glanced at him but said nothing. "Ok, then. Let's not waste time." Barrett looked at the cow. They were looking at each other. The cow remained blank. But it was peaceful, and the sun was streaming through the top of the trees. Barrett's hands moved down. He kneeled down and started stroking the cow's udder. Her body was responding. She looked up and glanced at him, remembering human touch, just letting him get on with it. The animal glanced at Barrett again, watching his head move. His hands seem to know what they were doing. Muscle memory. Growing up on a farm. It all came flashing back to him. It was something he had never done before, or so he had thought but he was wrong. The man and the little girl stared at him, wondering what he was doing, why the cow was not running. He still knelt and the cow just let him milk her. A lot of the milk ended up on the floor but there was enough left to fill the bottle the man had given him. Barrett just kept talking, smiling, milking, and the cow let him get on with it. Her friends looked on just like her calf. Everything seemed to be fine. Barrett still squatted and his legs started to ache but he was afraid of letting go of the animal. Maybe it would kick him instead of letting him take milk, milk that was meant to be for her calf. Barrett didn't know enough about these sorts of things. He couldn't remember. What he remembered was how they killed his grandmother. How they had been hiding at her farm but how it hadn't been away far enough for people not to find them. It had taken a long time but bad people had found them at some point. It was always about food. People were starving and sick, which turned them violent. Somehow he could understand that but they had also done other things to his mother and grandmother. Things that had nothing to do with being starving, that had killed his nanna and made the happy lights in his mother's eyes go out. As for food—well, these people took everything, all the fruits and vegetables and they had killed the pigs and cows.

While his hands were working Barrett remembered that his grandmother had been a very kind woman who had a lot of love to give to him and the world. He didn't remember her talking about his grandfather but then maybe he had been too young. He had only been five when they had left the farm or what was left of it. He remembers that his nanna had never sat still; she was always busy with her hands. And when she died, there was a big emptiness inside Barrett. But he didn't have time to cry for her, they had to run. Turning his back to the man and his girl who were still watching him, smiling, he cried. The tears were for his family whom he would never be with again. He would never milk another cow with his granny or listen to any of his mother's story. The boy would never raise hares or feed pigs with them or listen to one of his father's jokes again. They were gone. But somehow they would always be a part of him. Milking this cow was part of his grandmother and what she had taught him. There had been lots of farmers before they died of religious or other violence, radiation, explosions and illnesses like cancer but none of them had been like his granny. Nobody could be the way she was. They had barely been getting by, but their connection to each other had been deep. Even Barrett being not much more than a toddler had known this. They had been blissfully happy together, even though the world was breaking down around them. His grandmother had been very independent. She grew her own food; her electricity had come from solar and generators and she had lots of fuel in storage. Not relying on other people had always been some kind of obsession for her. Reality had caught up with her as well. It had just taken longer because she lived so far away from civilisation. Thoughts of protecting herself had never had a home in here. She just didn't like people and didn't want to see them. Obviously apart from her immediate family. And Barrett and his parents had just been lucky to spend a two-week holiday at her place, when everything around them went up in flames. He remembered his father and granny spending weeks analysing every possible outcome, their chances of surviving, having arguments and dismissing the misinformation. His father always wanted to go back, trusting in the good of people, expecting them to stick together. His grandmother and mother had always thought religion destroyed people and could bring out the worse in them. So, going back would be suicide unless you belonged to a radical religious group that could offer you some sort of protection. But to do that you would have to lie, hide your true self when it came to your own beliefs. Like the American president had, pretending he was a believer once he got sworn in. He lied, but it was an accepted form of lying. It was easier than the truth. A strategy to focus on survival and not your own happiness. These days were clearly over. But his granny always said they needed proof to make their story compelling. Make fundamentalists believe they supported their cause was hard work. Did they really give up the nice country life for something so challenging with no guarantee of anything? And of course, the illnesses. Cities bred them, once the sewage systems collapsed. His grandma had heard that these evil people now used the government's bombs. No-one was protecting them anymore. These people knew where the bombs were. How she could know that living away from everybody with no television, internet or phone was questionable. But the decision had been taken out of their hands because the people granny was afraid of had found them. Nobody could have prevented it. It was just a matter of time. Barrett turned around to the man and his girl. His future was with them now and the milk was the start. Even at his age he realised they would probably die. The nuclear weapons would destroy them all but at least he would not die on his own. And if there was a god, maybe that was his intention. For people, religious or not to destroy themselves, so he could create a new human race. Maybe god was just tired of being made responsible for everything that went wrong on earth, for having the finger pointed about every war that was going on. So maybe he made this the last one and have a bit of fun with it. Stretching it out. Somehow that was easier to stomach than the thought of nothing making sense at all. A small intervention by a supernatural force was better than a full accidental invasion by some stupid human beings in search of something that didn't even exist. Imagining a world in which there was no good seemed to be a very sad thought. Something that might be logical looking at everything that had happened so far but nothing that Barrett wanted to believe. Shishi stared at him. Barrett stopped milking the cow. He sighed sadly. Somehow he could have done this forever, just forgetting where he was. He turned his attention to the father. Both of them were still sitting on the other side of the stream. The man mouthed something. "Well done," he seemed to say. Barrett grinned. He slowly got up holding on to the bottle. Of course, there was a lot of milk on the ground but it didn't matter. The cow looked past him now towards her calf that was coming closer. Barrett didn't want to be close to the cow when her baby was there as well. Maybe she would suddenly turn against him. So, he just patted the animal a slowly walked back. One last look at the herd. Hopefully they would stay but they probably would move on. But the three of them had been given a new start. Maybe a new world was waiting for them. At least for a while. If they could keep the cows somehow they would have enough food to keep them alive and healthy without having to fight for food every day, fighting off illnesses all the time, vitamins or whatever it was called that kept the human body healthy, even if it wasn't going to last forever. It wasn't for keep. Sooner or later they would be found, either by other humans or by some wild animals. But everything was slowly dropping to pieces, anyway. If they wanted fresh stuff, they needed to grow it themselves and still slowly kill themselves with all the poison that would surely be in the plants. Maybe it was in the milk already. But what did it matter? He stepped through the stream now. The girl's father and Shishi walked towards him, smiling.

"We can have milk whenever we want to now." The girl was holding her dad's hand, skipping. "Barrett knows how to milk cows. We just need to make sure they don't run away."

"We could live like our ancestors did," the man smiled. They were looking at Barrett curiously. It was the first time they had met a young boy with real skills.

"Now," the man said. We have to decide how we keep them here. Maybe tie them down with a rope or something or maybe just one or two. The others probably stay nearby then, anyway. We can't take them home; that much is for sure. Somehow we have to think of them as a long-term investment."

"Not meat," Barrett added. They all nodded. The man looking gaunt, wiry and older than he was seemed to lighten up. There was a glimmer of hope in his eyes. He gazed across the stream at the animal grazing just a few feet away from them, his eyes sky-blue under thick dark brows. Maybe there was a chance he could share responsibly. Yes, the kids were very young. But in these days, age was just a number, anyway. He had seen kids younger than these do some horrendous things. "If we can just keep two and the calf," he said, "we can assume that we will have enough milk to get us over the winter and if everything fails, we always have their meat." The girl sucked her breath in sharply.

"We don't want to do that," Barrett added. "Only saying." His voice was quiet and firm. "We've got to plan. Have something like a backup plan. The girl was silent, biting her lip. She sighed. "I know."

"Sir," Barrett whispered. How can we make sure nobody or… nothing, you know some animal will take them if we leave them outside?"

"We can't."

"And how do you know they're healthy? I mean, you know. This radiation everybody is talking about."

"It's too late to worry about it now. People died. We survived. People are still dying, and we're still alive. Who knows? Maybe we'll be lucky."

"Is that luck?" the girl asked quietly. The man just frowned at her.

"Ok, enough of the depressing stuff," Barrett said forcefully. "Let's find something like a rope. God help us." The girl's mouth hung open, her eyes widening. "Is god going to help us?" The man snapped. When are you going to get it? God doesn't exist! He didn't create earth and heaven. There is no heaven, and there's no life after death! Stop behaving like there is. I'm sick and tired of this senseless belief in something supernatural." The girl said nothing but tears were running down her face. She didn't look up. Instead, she closed her eyes and took a deep breath, trying to calm herself. "Maybe, but it's a nice thought, isn't it?"

The man shook his head.

"I'm sorry I snapped. Barrett is right. I didn't sleep last night," he mumbled, looking at his daughter who had already calmed down.

"I know. But wouldn't it be nice if there was and one day we could all be happy?" She closed her mouth, sighed, dropping her hands to her sides. "It would be wonderful to be safe," the man said after a long while. Shishi turned, padded Sammy who had come back with a fan in his mouth and started walking. "We need to find a rope." Yes, the man thought. Safe. But it seemed there was only pain wherever he looked. Whenever he thought things would be better, something happened and someone took things from him. He didn't speak much for the next few minutes, except to give advice on what to do to making a rope. Finding some dead tree parts with bark hanging off was easy. They were lucky to have cedar. Flattening the stalk to break the core wood, separating it into two roughly equal halves. The man had done this a thousand times. The wood could be removed easily. He pretended not to care about what he had said to Shishi but he could have beaten himself to get carried away that much. He tried to concentrate on the rope making. Why had he burdened his little girl with his past? He tenderised the fibre by grinding it between his thumb and forefinger and then twisted the long section of fibre until it started to loop and kink. The kids were very quick in copying and soon they had something like a rope to work with. But the man's mind couldn't stop going back to the incident. He shouldn't have made her sad about something she had nothing to do with. She had been far too young and had enough to carry herself. He sat on the floor, pretending to look at something and stared at his hands until his eyes felt out of focus. He thought of a nice Sunday dinner and wondered if he would ever taste Yorkshire pudding again instead of eating raw plants. And he noticed, too, how he remembered things from his early childhood. Stuff he had thought his brain had buried in a place he could never get to again. He remembered his mother wearing makeup just for pleasure. Nobody did this anymore not even women who prostituted themselves. It wouldn't make any difference. Most men were too starving or sick to have any interest. In the early days, sure. But now? But how could he be sure? He hadn't been in the cities for years and he didn't want to. He thought about his mother sitting on the couch with him, laughing and touching his hair, stroking it. He wondered what he would do now if things would have been different. If there never would have been religion. Would it have made a difference or would people have killed each other anyhow, just for a different reason? He remembered how his father had talked to his mum after one of the political changes that had happened over the years and it had seemed to be a big thing but nothing to do with religion. Well, not directly anyway. Even though a lot of Muslim refugees seemed to be one reason of people being scared and voting for this Brexit.

He heard the voice of his father in his mind. "One thing's clear. England never got over losing its status as a world leader and having to be part of a European system, where it's only one country of many, important, but only one member among many. And this system dares to tell them it has to let in a lot of strangers into their country. Suddenly they can get out of it by having a partnership with the US. This was an opportunity for the American president. Old memories and dreams were awakening again. Actually, a lot of people hoped that they had overcome all this nonsense and that Europe would become a great new unity with Great Britain. But as you can see it is like fashion. Old forms, cuts, patterns and colours seem to come back. People like what they know, even if it's not good for them. And there's nothing more they are afraid of than things or people they don't know or understand. What remains is to acknowledge the realities and accept the consequences." Only now the man understood what his father had meant. The consequences were hate. That's just how people's minds worked. After the first days in shock people had gathered together with like-minded people following a simple pattern. Hating everyone who was different. Religion was a smoke screen. They had spent hunting down everyone who looked different. That was the easiest way. After all you couldn't look into people's heads, and when that had been done, they started to fight each other, whoever was the most radical. And now? What was left? Religion? Yes, somehow it had survived. But there weren't enough people left to spread the word. Unfortunately, there was no way of telling how many people had made it. The only way was to hide. Just in case. He looked at Barrett and smiled. There was hope. Hope for Shishi to live after her father was gone. After all, he had made a promise.

The next days and weeks just went by in a haze. In the mornings they explored the forest looking for edible things. The girl taught Barrett about the medical side-effects of some plants. Cliff continued to deteriorate, but he seemed to be happy where he was, looking forward to meeting his god. The man just let him dream. Sometimes they went hunting in the hills. Barrett had shown them how to catch little rabbits. They dined inside, having fires during the day, and discovered soon how they could lead the smoke far away from their underground house. And gradually, without many words, they taught each other trust. They were accustomed to look behind them every second, being scared expecting the worst, wild animals, angry people. But nothing happened. The cows stayed. They had tied down one of them, but with a long rope, so it could move around comfortably, and the others just stayed with their friend. A week passed, then another and another.

One day they woke together, got up and prepared to go out to milk the cow. Cliff hadn't. He lied in his bed, stiff and cold, with his arms beside him. Cancer had finally eaten away the last bit of life left in him. They buried him after breakfast noting the tension and a strange sense of loss, but they had lost too many people they cared about to be devastated. Twenty-four hours later, they were all going about their routine tasks. "Is he in heaven now?" Shishi asked at one point, looking at a stinging nettle. "Cliff, I mean."

"Maybe," her father answered continuing to fill up bottles with water from the stream.

"I'm sure he is," Barrett murmured.

"But if god wanted him, why did he let him get poisoned by this radiation and get infected? Why didn't he take him quickly?" The man grew frustrated. He wanted to talk about what he had been through and why god had let that happen, but then they all had suffered. It was pointless. Shishi would find out the answer herself when she was ready. But so far she'd been unable to accept that there was no god. She just kept questioning it, trying to find a loophole how he could exist and be a merciful god, even though he let all these things happen. Something was ruffling the bushes. They all turned around. Barrett stepped out with Sammy behind him. He looked like he'd been doing twenty rounds with a prize boxer. "What the hell happened to you?" the man asked. "Tried to find the cows," he answered with a shaky voice, before explaining that he had walked through the stream to milk the one cow that always let him despite her calf. The girl had walked off to find some herbs, and edible plants and the man seemed busy with setting up slings for the rabbits. "So, the rope didn't hold, and they walked off then?"

"I'm not sure. I couldn't see the rope. But something did… let it loose," he said.

"Don't worry. We were just trying anyway. It's not your fault. I think we should go and just have a look. Maybe I can help you, and we find them again. If they just wandered off, they might still be near."

"I don't think they just… wondered off," the boy said with a shaking voice. "And I'm not sure if I want to go back." The man didn't answer straight away. Only looked at him, frowning. "Let's go. I want to see myself. Or actually. Maybe you want to make sure Shishi is ok. Find her. She's just over there." The man pointed at the girl's red coat in the bushes. "I consider myself a big boy. So, I'm sure I can find them myself."

"Or what's left," Barrett whispered under his breath.

"Pardon."

"Nothing, I'll find Shishi. We'll wait here."

"Sure, Barrett. You're not afraid of something, are you?"

"Not in the least. I'm just not sure what happened." His eyes were red. But he seemed to have himself under control. The man walked towards the stream, looking slowly and methodically around, waited. Dead silence. Well, apart from the wind and the birds. Strange how the birds always survived.

"You're okay?" Barrett asked loudly.

"Sure. Don't worry. Get Shishi."

"Course." Barrett smiled and walked towards the girl. He was determined to join her. She was smiling a little now, oblivious to what was going on around here. The dog just wagged his tail and continued sniffing something interesting on the floor. He didn't know what had happened to the cows, or maybe he just wasn't interested. "What happened to you?" she asked.

I just walked through the bushes to have a look at our cow and just ran back when it wasn't there?"

"Oh, were you scared?"

"Yes."

"I'm not. I feel safe here. They just walked off. Didn't like the grass, maybe. Sammy would have barked if it was something dangerous."

"Are you sure?"

"Yes." Maybe the girl was right, and Barrett had panicked for nothing. He hadn't heard gunshots, the growling of wild animals or worse. People had used more powerful nova bombs before. He had never seen them, but he had seen the consequences on people and animals. People had stopped using them because the stuff to fire them up was unstable in large quantities. His dad had told him. These rockets tended to explode while they were still on the way to their destination, so terrorists had stopped using them. But Barrett remembered the noises they made. And he remembered the burned bodies and the smell. There was no smell of charred meat here. Maybe the cows had just walked away, or perhaps someone had taken them, but this somebody was a proper person just like them.

"What was she like?"

"Who?"

"Your mother?" Shishi looked at him with her big eyes.

"Why?"

"I don't know. I've never met mine. I don't know if she could milk cows. I wish I could ask her."

Why don't you ask your dad?"

"He doesn't like talking about her."

"Oh," Barrett thought a minute, twiddling a small piece of wood between his fingers. "I remember her, my mother. She was lovely. In my mind, I can see her wearing her hair in a bun to keep it out of her face, standing with her feet apart, leaning forward having a go at my granny. I've almost forgotten how she stood like. She seemed like the most beautiful mum in the world to me then. But I was too little when she died. So, when we were at the farm, I was even smaller. I don't suppose she was a farmer. She just adapted. Who knows, she might have lived to like it if cholera hadn't killed her." Barrett moved a bit and sat down on a rotten tree stump. Suddenly his eyes widened. "What?", the girl asked.

"Sh…", Barrett put a finger to his lips and got up, pushing the bushes aside in front of him.

The bodies of a man and two women laid in the ditch. They all looked dead. Next to them was a cow's head. The girl shrieked, slipped and scrambled down towards them, inspecting them. "Come back here," Barrett hissed. "They might not be dead."

"They are."

"Ok, but we don't know what they died of. It might be contagious."

"I think it was some animal. They're all scratched and bloody. It only left the cow's head."

The girl ducked back down. "Why did they leave the cow's head? Because it's not pretty?" Barrett laughed. "Maybe?" She hesitated. "I know you saw something over there. You just didn't want to tell dad. Why not?" She wished that she'd said something different, anything but to tell him he had been lying. But it was too late, and she was scared. He looked at her. "I don't want things to change. I like it here?"

"What d'you mean here?"

Barrett blushed, and it looked completely out of place. He was just a young boy. However, he had always seemed so strong. But now, the colour in his cheeks showed his real age. "Everything was so peaceful. Even Cliff. I know he died, but it was quiet, and he wasn't scared, and you looked after him. You have a house that can't be found easily, and there aren't many people here, and then we found the cows. I just... I hoped... I don't know."

"I know what you mean, and now everything seems to change again, right?"

"Yes."

"We're here," she mumbled. "You're not alone."

She had come to an abrupt stop and was gazing at the dead people in the ditch. She had seen so many of them in her short life. "But this is it. That's life. It's changing all the time. But as long as we all have each other. You know, you, me and dad. He will look after us."

You're sure?" She nodded. But you have to tell me what you saw. He looked up again. "They didn't have any guns, and they did nothing threatening. But these... they didn't stop at all, just kept going and going. I just watched it in silence. Couldn't do anything. I was so scared. I'm scared of people, of certain people but sometimes you can reason with them. These animals don't understand us. They just attack. You cannot reason with them." The girl just looked at him. "What do you mean?"

"It was late in the day. But it wasn't dark yet. You know I had gone out again because I wanted to get some more milk. You had asked me if you could come, but your dad wanted you to stay and learn more about this medical stuff he's always going on about. You had promised you would cook us a nice meal when I came back."

"Yes, I know. We had peppermint leaves and rabbit. It was lovely, but it took you ages to eat. You were quiet, and dad had asked you if you were ok." I know, and it was nice, but I kept going over and over what I had seen. I kept contemplating about the weapons these people had. Knives, axes, picks, guns. I'm not sure what they used it for. You know, people or animals. Did they use it for slaughtering? It scared me when I saw them. And they were all so thin and smiled. But not at me. They didn't see me. I was hiding in the bushes."

"What?", The girl sounded confused. Barret walked over to the stream, kneeled down and put his whole head underwater. When he emerged again, he pulled his dripping hair back with both hands and sighed. "I know, you have no idea what I'm talking about."

"Well… I'm not sure." She looked at her, and he saw something in her eyes, a look of what? Memory? As if she knew what he had seen?

Barret told her he had taken the man's gun and had headed off into the woods.

"What do you mean you had taken dad's gun?"

"I mean I just took it. I don't know why… just had a strange notion something might happen, and I got out and walked over there." He pointed to the stream and the patch of grass the cows had been grazing on. "Right there."

"But he didn't know?" It seemed a logical question; her dad had said nothing, but maybe she just didn't know. Perhaps he had.

"Probably not. He has said nothing to me, and I put it back after I used it."

"It was a pretty loud bang. I thought he would hear it."

"What?"

"How did you… you followed me?" She bit her lip. "I didn't mean to. Sam ran after you. He was running ahead of me and didn't listen when I called him back. So, I followed him. And when I saw you again trailing into the bush and wading through the stream, I watched. I wasn't scared. Only curious."

"How much did you see?" She just looked at him. It had started to rain, turning into a downpour. "And why didn't you tell your dad?"

"The dead people were here. He won't find anything where he's going and… I think I saw most of it. I could hear the shouting. I just wasn't sure how far away they were? Did they see you? I was holding on to Sam. He wanted to run and protect you. I just sat there and then the fight started. You know these two men and the woman. They dragged her to the ground. But I couldn't see what they were doing. She screamed, but it didn't last long."

"I know what they did. I was close enough. But it was getting darker, and I was scared as well. If you were there you know, I turned around and wanted to walk back. They had killed the cows, but it was three of them. I couldn't have done anything."

"I know. And the man was fighting among them. I could only hear the shouting, not what they were shouting about."

"It was the meat."

"The cows?"

"That as well." The girl frowned but didn't ask. "You just took one small step at a time, keeping it as quiet as you could."

"It wasn't enough."

"I know. You don't need to worry."

"Your dad will notice."

"How?"

"He counts the bullets."

"He hasn't used his gun for ages."

"He still counts the bullets sometimes." The girl nodded and said nothing. All the while it continued to rain. They looked up. The girl put out her tongue to catch the raindrops.

The boy listened to the rain drumming in the upper parts of the forest, dripping down the tree leaves. "So, you killed them."

"Only one. The other killed himself accidently," Barrett said, "You were there. He dripped over the dead woman and broke his neck. I think it was a tree stump, but I didn't look."

"There are lots of dead people around at the moment," the girl mumbled.

"There always have been."

"Do you think it will ever change?"

The rain had died. Barret looked at her. He felt tired, like on the dawn edge of sleep, not yet ready to go to bed. After all, they had to go back to the house. He jerked awake, yawning, waiting for Shishi's father to come back. "Maybe it will change. People must be tired of wanting to kill each other. Or maybe they will just be too weak." He turned to the girl. Let's find some firewood and some food, while we wait." He could hear her breathing fast, then slower. "Ok." The sun was touching the tops of the trees with its orange paintbrush. The air still smelled of winter.

London September 2020
Mark and Benazir

He could be dying. He was ready. But he couldn't do it. Not with Benazir being behind him. He could tell him to get Aisha. Take her… but Barbara would catch them and keep her! Christian or not. Or whatever religion they were practising. He couldn't get out. Luck wasn't on his side. These women would do whatever she asked them to do. And he would be dead before he could reach the latch. But he couldn't spend another night with them. Not with her. Not with that woman. The end was coming anyway. But there was one more option. Tell Ben and try to escape when everybody was asleep. But one disturbing fact would remain. He would have to be with Barbara again. He didn't think he could do that. The thought of her touch made him feel sick again. Last night was behind him now, but he could still feel her everywhere on his body. Soon there would be darkness again. It was almost morning but the day would go fast, too fast. Maybe he could kill her. Maybe when she was asleep, lying next to him. With her death, Mark would be free. It wouldn't matter what happened to him afterwards. Maybe they would understand. Perhaps they were decent women and would understand. These women whose families, whose life had been destroyed by a senseless war that had no winners. A fight that had seen so many deaths since the atomic bomb North Korea had detonated to show the American president he wasn't in control. "Praise the Lord", one woman suddenly screamed, and Mark knew he was wrong. They would never understand if he killed one of them. "Ben," he called to his friend. Mark carefully scanned the room, checking his weapon. He would leave within the next few minutes, one way or another, with Ben or without him. But he would give him a chance to choose. Mark felt like he had died once when this woman touched him, and he would die again if he would have to spend one more night with her. He was ready. He lowered himself on a crate and waited for Ben to walk over again. He could smell the surrounding paint, penetrating his nostrils, informing him of the waste of time these women were experiencing every day. The senselessness of bringing babies into this world, when the living was being killed every day. Time was running out. Ben stood in front of him now, holding Aisha. "What?", he just said. "Tell me. I can take it. I know something is wrong."

"We need to leave. I can't stay here."

"Why?"

"She touched me."

"What? Who?"

"Barbara."

Ben smiled. He didn't understand. "So? And?" She touched me as well. She shook my hand, and I didn't pull away like they taught me at home if a woman touches me. It's not that bad. Trust me."

"Not that touching."

"What d'you mean? Not that touching. What sort?"

"Mark took a deep breath. "Last night. When everyone was asleep. Has nobody come over to you and… woke you up?"

"No, but I sleep very heavily."

"Well, I was woken up. She… she reached for my…"

"Your what?"

"You know."

"No, I don't." Mark just looked at him.

"Oh, Allah. That's disgusting."

Mark realised why he had felt the compulsion not to tell his friend. He was back in the dark room, which he had tried to forget but couldn't. He could feel Barbara's touch again. Ben's expression had reminded him of that fragment of memory. It made him feel sick. All he could do was not to shiver.

"Do you think she will do it again?", Ben asked quietly.

"Yes. She said she wants a baby."

"Yaks. You're only thirteen. Is that even possible?"

"I don't know, and I don't care."

"You want to leave tonight?", Ben just said.

"What?"

"Tonight? We can't leave now. It would be too obvious. I could lay next to you so that she won't come over. Where is she now?"

"I don't know. Hell, maybe?"

"That would be nice", Ben smiled. "But I doubt it." He sighed. "She seemed to be such a lovely kind woman, with her quiet low voice and she seemed to have an answer to everything."

"D'you think I'm lying?"

"No."

"She's not what she seems to be."

"I know. I think we have to leave tonight, but we have to take baby formula. We're not safe, and Aisha is not safe. Strange. It seems years ago when everything was ok."

"It wasn't that long ago. But it feels longer. We watched our world fall apart. Guess that ages you, and you lose sense of time. Everything we knew was gone in less than a few hours."

"There's no safety." Ben just made a statement. It wasn't a question.

Mark still answered. "No." In his memory, distorted by a young boys' sense of time, it felt like an eternity. All he remembered was that it was such a peaceful, relaxing time. They had just gone to school, rode bikes, played computer games, watched rockets being fired by North Korea on the internet. But it hadn't seemed real. No, this was real. Life was crap. And the future didn't exist. There was only surviving the next day. "Tonight," Ben said.

"Tonight?"

"Yes, tonight. I will try to get to the baby formula somehow. "

During the following hour, they talked about a lot of things, and Ben learned a lot more than he wanted to know. "Ok" he just said. "I have to distract them and get food for Aisha. Maybe I can steal some apples. They are in that little corner over there. It's hidden from everyone's view. That's where they store the formula too." Mark's friend was amazing. He just took action. He seemed to understand how staying was worse for Mark than dying. And for him, it was more important to stay together even if it meant being on the streets again.

"Why?"

Ben just looked at Mark, a frown creasing his forehead. "What d'you mean, why?"

"I mean. Why are you doing this for me? You could stay. They would let you. You could pretend to be a Christian. You're good at it. You said so yourself. You could be safe."

"I wouldn't be safe and Aisha wouldn't. If they can do this to you, they could kill me for not being a good enough Christian. And I don't want Aisha to be a breeding machine when she's old enough. At least I can look after her on the streets."

Someone opened the door to the storage hall. Both boys turned their heads. It was Barbara. Mark saw a crack of candlelight under the door. But it was closed pretty quick. She walked over to them, behaving as if nothing had happened the night before. The woman smiled, and when she was close enough, she put her hand on Ben's shoulder. The other women started singing some religious songs, and she continued to smile, moving her body in some imaginary rhythm. The singing stopped. "Continue, sisters", she shouted. They obeyed.

"They do what you tell them to do," Ben stated as a matter of fact. His face didn't give away anything.

"Well, I don't want to be the leader, but the Lord has somehow chosen me. How can I not accept?"

Ben just shrugged. "I guess."

"What are you guys talking about?," she asked, biting her lip. The room went dark. Nobody spoke until candlelight suddenly illuminated it. But it had taken the woman quite a long time to light every one of them. A few of the women had prepared for an event like this. "Let's pray," someone shouted for no clear reason. Barbara didn't have a candle of her own. Ben and Mark looked at each other. Finally, Ben spoke. "Does this happen often?"

"What?" Barbara was confused.

"That the lights go off."

"About once a day." Barbara said, softly, "The generator doesn't work properly anymore. The Lord will switch it on again, if we need it, Ben."

"Amen", he answered.

"Amen," all the women shouted.

Mark started plucking at the front of his jeans. There were holes in them, but he didn't care. He would soon grow out of them. Barbara just smiled at them and walked off without saying another word.

"I know what you think", Mark whispered.

"It will not work."

"I know. It's too unpredictable. And we wouldn't have enough time. Only one candle needs to be lit, and they would see where we're going."

Marks' face went blank. "I have another idea."

"Tell me."

"You won't like it. "

"Tell me."

"It puts all of us in danger."

"We are in danger."

"What if Aisha dies and we'll survive?"

"That will not happen."

"How d'you know?"

"If she dies I will," Ben said simply. "So, tell me about your plan.

"Fire."

"What?"

"Fire. A fire. I mean look around you. Nothing will stay behind. They will burn everything."

"Mark, are you ok? I mean what the hell are you talking about?"

"Why aren't you getting it. There's no way we can leave at night. We're too far at the back, and they always have someone guarding. We can't run and make it up that ladder when the lights go off. But imagine starting a fire with all these candles. Look around you. It's a miracle they haven't burned down this place already. Everything is wood. There's newspaper everywhere, wooden crates and curtains. Look at all these curtains. God knows what they need them for. There are no windows."

"There's just one exit. And they would panic."

"I know. We could die."

"They destroyed cities."

"What?"

Ben looked at him. "They destroy everything. We have to start somewhere else, and it cannot be here. So, what does it matter if we die?"

Mark said nothing.

"Look," Ben said. "At us, I mean. At them. Maybe it's better if we die. It will not be better outside. There's just one chance… See? We either make or not. If we do, maybe there's a god. If we die… what, does it matter? Mark turned to at the women again, craning his neck one way then the other to get a good look at the room. After a few moments, he sighed, turned back to Ben, a look of desperation on his face. If we make it, where will we go?"

"The forest," Ben smiled. Mark smiled back at him. "The forest?"

"The forest." They could hear the clang of feet approaching and looked up to see Barbara.

"What's in the forest?" Barbara asked who had tried to sneak up from behind. Ben just smiled. Only Mark knew how scared he was. "We were just talking about how much we loved the forest when we were little because we lived in the city. Our parents used to take us there sometimes. But we think it's all burned now."

"Yes, it is," Barbara said. I spoke to a few friends. They told me there is not much forest left. Nothing near London anyway. Apparently, some bombs went off, and that was it. We could feel the vibration. It wasn't nice, but we prayed to god, and everything turned out alright. Ben looked at Mark rolling his eyes. Only now they realised Barbara was holding a gun in her right hand. But she wasn't pointing it at them. "You boys," she said, her voice loud and stronger. "You are better off here. It's safer. Safer for you and Allie." She undoubtedly knew something was up, but she hadn't heard what they had been talking about. "The Lord knows who we are. He has plans for us, and he wants us to stay here for now. "We will run out of food at some point,"

Mark whispered. She smiled, but there was no reply. She looked at him and sighed. "You're the man now. Here, I mean. You believe in the Lord, and he will provide for you and us. He's been watching you. He knows everything we… you are doing. "Mark was silent. His hands were shaking. "She smiled slyly. I think it's time for our daily prayer. Will you join us?" "Of course," Ben smiled. We will join you in one moment. It's in the church, right?"

"The church. She frowned. Her confusion changed into a big grin. The church. I like that. Yes, it's in the church over there." She pointed at the curtain. "That's exactly what I meant," Ben said dryly. I think it's time for Allie's feed. I will do that, and then the three of us will join you.

"Well, Mark can come with me now, and you can follow as soon as you finish."

"No," Mark shouted. Ben touched his arm. "What he means… what Mark means is, he will need to hold Allie while I prepare the formula. I'm still a bit unsure about it all. My mum used to do it."

"One of my girls can help you."

"Don't worry. Mark has helped me before, and I'm sure the girls can't wait to worship our Lord," Ben said firmly. "We'll see you in about ten minutes. As you said, we're the men now. We'll be fine." She looked uneasy but just nodded and walked off.

"Ok," Ben said.

"Ok, what?" Mark looked at him with a confused look on his face. Ben took a deep breath. "Don't you understand? It's now or never."

"What if it's a mistake?" Mark choked.

"Well, we'll soon find that out. It looks like luck is on our side. They store the candles next to the baby formula. And we have a reason to go there." Ben pointed to a shelf on his left side. Ben looked up, worried but somehow hopeful. "Ok. So, you have a good plan?"

"No."

"Oh."

"I just hope."

"That's good enough for me."

"Let's feed Aisha. If we all die… well, at least we have all this crap behind us. Don't they say in death, all things become clear?"

"We're not going to die. I asked Allah," Ben smiled shyly. "Let's go." Mark nodded and just followed his friend. He felt a sharp clarity he'd never known. If they died, he wouldn't mind. The woman and her religion were of no comfort. If there was no god everything would be ok. There would be no need for faith.

"Ok, Aisha. Darling. It's time for some early dinner," Benazir took his little sister and placed her in Mark's arms. "Hold her for one second, "he said.

"We'll struggle to look after your sister."

"It makes no difference. Would be the same here."

The cruellest of fates had brought them here, but they had no choice. A handful of women walked past them, walking over, pushing the curtains aside and letting it fall shut behind them. They were as alone as they could be under the circumstances. Ben put his index finger on his lips. He had mixed the formula and handed over the bottle to Mark. "OK, where are the candles?", He whispered. Mark toyed with just creating a big explosion, but this would not work, not with candles. The one thing he didn't wish to do was to kill Ben and his sister Aisha.

"We have to hurry," Ben urged. "Look at these curtains over there. If we set them alight, they will start burning within seconds and create a lot of smoke. It will create chaos. The ladder is still up there on the latch. I found one of these baby rucksacks. It's perfect for carrying Aisha. I put some apples in this plastic bag." He lifted something up that looked like a grocery shopping bag, while he added two boxes of baby formula. He had done everything possible but what Mark wanted most was his mum. But she could never comfort him again, to tell him everything would be ok. Mark could hear the religious chanting behind the curtain. It chilled him to the bones. He couldn't go back there. "Let's go," he said. It felt like everything would overwhelm him. But Ben and his sister deserved a chance. He took the candle and the matches his friend was handing him and started to walk. The cellar seemed much bigger, and its sheer immensity seemed to suffocate him. But he made it. Something else took over his mind. The fire eating the curtains was burning greedily within seconds when he had put a match to it. Thick smoke developed. He only turned around to see if Ben and Aisha were behind him. Once he was sure of it he started running, the smoke filling the room. He could hear the women's confused voices. He kept running and clambered awkwardly up the steps of the ladder until he had reached the latch and placed a hand on the handle pushing it up. It was easier than he had thought. In his mind, it had seemed so hard. Now he wished he would have tried it earlier. When his nose breathed in fresh air, he felt like being born again. He turned around to help Ben, making sure he could get out safely as well. Ben's head was just a few centimetres behind Mark's feet. "Look," he breathed. Ben lifted the carrier with his baby sister, trying to hand it to Mark. "Help me, will you?"

"Sure, just make sure you leave the latch open. These women need a chance. I don't want to kill them."

"But you don't want to be with them either."

"Correct.", Mark smiled bitterly while taking the carrier with Aisha from Ben. "Hurry," Ben suddenly screamed. "They're right behind me. They're pulling the ladder." Mark put the carrier and the plastic bag next to him on the ground and reached down with his hand to help his friend. Even though Mark was already outside, it was getting hard to breathe. The smoke was burning his nostrils. "Help me," Ben screamed. Please. Someone's pulling at my leg. I can't hold on." He started to slide down. A great wave of emotion swept over Mark. "Hold on," I have you. I won't let you go." He reached one hand down and grabbed Ben's left hand. But his friend was too slippery with sweat. They both coughed struggling to breathe. The screams of women pierced their ears. "Do you hear them?" Ben breathed. "They're dying."

"You will die if you don't pull yourself up. Hold on, come on."

"You will stay here. Here with us. We will stay together. And if the Lord wants us to die we'll all die, you little…." Barbara's voice sounded stretched and furious, not at all like the soft woman she had pretended to be. Ben just clung on to Mark's hand, kicking at the angry woman holding on to his foot but it was of no use. She didn't let go.

"I got you, Ben," Mark called out, but wasn't strong enough. And the fire was raging. Tears were streaming down his face while he could hear all the women screaming in pain. The air was dense with smoke, and the smell of burned flesh and hair hit his nose. It was a familiar smell. He wouldn't have paid attention to it anymore if he didn't know where it came from. He had to save Ben. He couldn't look after Aisha on his own. He was only thirteen. He realised the mistake he had made. Ben should have climbed out first. He should have been sitting here, at the entrance of the cellar with Aisha. But it was too late.

Because of the angle he was looking down at, he could only see Ben's head. He just assumed Barbara was still holding on even though her ranting and raving had stopped. He wasn't sure if the women were still screaming and he just couldn't hear them or if they had died. He remembered somewhere he'd heard that smoke inhalation killed more people than actual fires. Suddenly there was Ben pulling again. His hand jerked, and his eyes opened wide. "Take care of Aisha," he screamed, and his hand slipped from Mark's. Mark screamed until his voice was hoarse, but he couldn't hear himself. He felt deaf, his eardrums as insensate as bits of dead meat. He leaned forward as quick as he could, opened and closed his mouth, swallowed and forced air into his lung. A coughing fit prevented him from bending down any further. He could smell the fire, and he could hear the voices again. He just curled up in a ball until he could breathe again. Ben was gone.

He just sat at the latch until the fire forced him to move. Aisha started crying. What if someone would hear her? What would should they do? Scream and run? Well, Aisha couldn't run, but she could scream pretty well. Attack, with a baby in his arms? Ben was gone, and the cellar women had died with him. He couldn't sit here forever, and it was his fault that Ben had died. Mark needed to keep his promise to look after Aisha. But it had always been Ben who had made the important decisions. It didn't matter. His friend was not here anymore. Mark was alone. He couldn't trust anyone. Nobody would open their arms to him with love and look after him. There would always be a hidden agenda. One way or another, they would probably be killed. They only had one chance. Mark had to get out of the city and learn how to look after them himself. To feed and to keep them alive. He peered around. Four people were sitting around a fire a bit further away. They had guns but hadn't seen him, minding their own business. The screaming of the women hadn't bothered them. They were used to screams like everyone by now. They were skinny and tired-looking. Three men in filthy khakis and a woman in some dress but maybe it was just an ill-fitting t-shirt that had seen better days. She could have been pretty before she had lost her soul. Her age was difficult to guess. Maybe she could… No, women could not be trusted. They were no better than man. When Mark strained his eyes to look closer, he thought they all looked pretty wasted, anyway. And what did it matter? He would just get up and walk, be carrying Aisha until he would break down or someone killed them. He would feed her until he ran out of food. She would eat solids soon, so it should be easier. They would probably die before but he had promised Ben to try. Take care of her," Ben had said, and Mark had agreed. Except for the fact that he hadn't assumed it would be possible for Ben to die and leave him alone with Aisha. The baby just looked at him with trust in her eyes. Nobody was going to help him. Nobody. He started to cry. Ben's death, the way he had died and the responsibility he burdened Mark with, hung like a heavyweight in his stomach. He looked at Aisha who was still staring at him with her big brown eyes. Mark sighed. "I guess whatever Barbara said, she was right with one thing. I could become a father." He got up, reached down to the little girl and picked her up. "Where do you want to go? You don't know? Well, what about the forest? It's far, I think. But don't you think the forest sounds nice?"

Ross-on-Wye, Herefordshire
2026

"D'you know, what?", Shishi blurted.

"No, what?" Barret smiled.

"Shishi isn't my real name. It's just a nickname."

"I figured as much. It would be a strange name. What's your real name?"

"Dad doesn't want me to say it out loud. He says, some people wouldn't like it, because it's Muslim."

"Muslim?"

"Yes, it's a religion, like Cliff's. Different. But Muslim's believe in the same god."

"I know, what a Muslim is, but you and your dad don't seem to be very religious."

"We're not. But my mum was, and she gave me that name."

"What was your mum like?"

"I don't know. Dad doesn't talk about it."

"Maybe it makes him sad."

"Yes, I think it does."

"So, what's your real name?" She frowned. Barret put a hand on her shoulder. I'm sure you can tell me. There's no-one listening. Only the trees."

The girl leaned against a birch tree behind her. "I guess you're right. It's Aisha."

"That's a nice name," Barret breathed. He didn't pay attention being distracted by a movement behind Aisha. Sammy started to bark, disappearing into the bushes. "What the hell… He blinked, trying to focus properly. The man snorted. "It's just me." The girl shrieked. "You're back, daddy."

"Yes, pumpkin. I'm back."

"And did you find anything," she sang, jumping around him."

"Yes, I did," he looked at Barret. "But it's all gone now. Nobody has been left." Barret knew better. There was always someone or something left. "You don't need to pretend everything is fine."

"It's fine for now. But the cows are gone."

"That doesn't matter," Aisha cried. You're still the best daddy in the world." She picked up some stones from the ground. Barret didn't know what else to say and just looked at the man's bleeding hand. It was odd but from one moment to the next everything seemed to be ok. Dangerous as the world was, Barret thought it was possible that they would survive. He would learn from Aisha's father how to kill animals. They could build another underground house and another and another after that. And they would just invite nice people to stay with them. They could even build an underground hospital. They would heal people's minds and their bodies. The forest would provide them with all the herbs and plants they needed, and Aisha's dad would provide the knowledge. His spirit had woken up again. And when he looked at Aisha, he realised he had been feeling sad for too long. Forcing himself to breathe deeply, taking in the scents of the forest, he turned, walking back home. "Let's go home."

"Lets," said Aisha's dad. Barret appreciated that the surreal nightmares that he had had for so long would not disappear, but he could cope with them now. The man's cuts and bruises would heal, of course, the scars—both internal and external—would remain. But that was ok.

Suddenly Barret stopped and turned around. He shouted at the two people behind him. "Do you know what? You never told me your name, sir."

The man smiled. "My name's Mark."

Epilogue

The world's crisis had lasted for almost ten decades now. Diseases, war, hunger and above all, anarchy, had killed millions of people. It wasn't clear what had started it and why the world was still standing. Was it something small, that had gained momentum or had it been some big event like the American and the North Korean leaders finally using their atomic bombs instead of just using it as a threat? It didn't matter. They were all dead now. Mark gritted his teeth. It was time for him leave. He looked around. His head felt almost too heavy to move. Aisha sat at the end of his bed. She was a beautiful young woman now. "Is it time?", she asked with tears in her eyes. Mark nodded. All he wanted was to sleep, resting his tired body and not wake up again. He tried to speak, but it was too hard. He couldn't rise. He tried a second time. "Barret is a good guy."

"I know", she said, blushing.

"He will look after you."

"I don't need looking after."

"I know."

Tears filled her eyes. "Dad, why can't we heal cancer?"

"Maybe we're not meant to heal it."

"Because god doesn't want us to?"

"There is no…"

"Dad, don't… You don't know that."

He tried desperately to hold on to his consciousness. His strength lifted with the love she was oozing. But he had to tell her. "Aisha, I'm not your dad."

She just smiled; her lips were twitching as if she was trying to hold back a sob. "I know… I mean I didn't, but I guessed. You're so young. But for me you always will be. What happened to my real dad?" Mark's lower lip shook. "He got killed. Well, he kind of took his own life. I've never met him or your mum." The young woman sighed. "Why, I mean… Is Aisha my real name. I mean if you've never met my parents… how do you know…?

"I knew your brother. He was… he became my best friend.

"What happened to him and my mum? Do you know?"

He recalled happy times, remembering his childhood, his parents and his brother. He told Aisha how it had all started and why he looked after her, when her brother had died. How he remembered Ben and that his friend was the reason he had built this place with like-minded people in the forest instead of just waiting for death to take them. People who were tired of fighting. He told her Ben would always be there in spirit and when he looked at her, he could see that she was just like her brother, kind and full of hope.

Memories of joy flooded through Mark. "He was the best friend I've ever had, and he wanted to become an Imam. He wanted to help people, just like me. He had faith and there was nothing wrong with it. Not the way he did it."

***

Dear Reader, if you enjoyed "The sky above" please take a few moments to leave a review or rating on Amazon or Goodreads, but even if you didn't, I'm thankful for a review, as it helps me to understand what I can do better, to promote the book and to give other potential readers an insight into what they might be getting into. n.

www.ingramcontent.com/pod-product-compliance
Lightning Source LLC
Chambersburg PA
CBHW070653100726
47907CB00007B/2192